A Cultivated Crime

Grace Marcello

AnniesFiction.com

Books in the Victorian Mansion Flower Shop Mysteries series

A Fatal Arrangement
Bloomed to Die
The Mistletoe Murder
My Dearly Depotted
Digging Up Secrets
Planted Evidence
Loot of All Evil
Pine and Punishment
Herbal Malady
Deadhead and Buried
The Lily Vanishes
A Cultivated Crime
Suspicious Plots
Weeds of Doubt
Thorn to Secrecy
A Seedy Development
Woes By Any Other Name
Noel Way Out
Rooted in Malice
Absent Without Leaf
Dormant Lies
Best Laid Plants
Pocket Full of Deadly
To Hive and to Hold

A Cultivated Crime

Library of Congress-in-Publication Data
A Cultivated Crime / by Grace Marcello
p. cm.
I. Title
2018949441

AnniesFiction.com
(800) 282-6643
Victorian Mansion Flower Shop Mysteries™
Series Creators: Shari Lohner, Janice Tate
Editor: Lorie Jones
Cover Illustrator: Bob Kayganich

10 11 12 13 14 | Printed in South Korea | 9 8 7 6 5 4 3

1

"When a woman is murdered, they should always look at the husband first," DeeDee Wilcox declared.

Kaylee Bleu shook her head. She had to hand it to DeeDee to sound like such an expert on the morbid subject.

"Even if he's tied up and unconscious in the basement?" Jessica Roberts asked doubtfully.

"Especially then." DeeDee leaned forward, shoving aside her half-eaten chocolate croissant. The topic was apparently compelling enough to make her forget about one of her favorite pastimes—eating anything chocolate—which they were all doing this morning at Jessica's decadent bakery and coffee shop, Death by Chocolate.

DeeDee ran Between the Lines, a mystery bookstore, and therefore had ample opportunity to read about murders of all kinds, often before the rest of them. This morning she was filling them in on her latest read.

"The book paints the guy as a saint. But what kind of man lets his wife and two daughters get kidnapped while he sits on a couch with his hands allegedly tied? I mean, come on. That's a huge red flag." DeeDee turned to Kaylee. "Can you imagine Reese doing anything like that? He'd fight to the death to protect someone he loves."

Kaylee felt her face redden. Naturally, DeeDee had to use Reese Holt as the best example of a courageous man. A master carpenter who ran his own business, Reese was the whole package—kind, strong, handsome, and handy. He was the most sought-after handyman in Turtle Cove, Washington, and he received a good deal of attention from the women in town.

Kaylee couldn't argue with DeeDee's logic, but her friend was being blatantly obvious about the fact that she wanted Kaylee to fall into Reese's arms.

Since Kaylee had moved to the area, she'd gotten to know Reese. He was always on hand to help her with any repairs or improvements, whether at The Flower Patch or Wildflower Cottage, where she and her dachshund, Bear, lived. She'd bought the shop and the cottage from her grandmother a few years ago, and Reese had always helped her grandmother too. Kaylee and Reese were just friends—nothing more.

"He does seem like the type to put up a fight," Kaylee said lamely.

"Oh, I think he'd do more than put up a fight," Mary Bishop, the fourth member of their group, said with a mischievous smile. "Especially if it was Kaylee."

"I don't need some guy to save me," Kaylee argued. "Can we get back to the oh-so-cheery topics of home invasions and kidnapping? Or better yet, gardening?"

After all, that was their purpose. The four women belonged to the Petal Pushers garden club. Theoretically, they talked about gardening. Realistically, they chatted about gardening and any other interesting—or creepy—topic that struck their fancy.

The Petals loved mysteries, and they would never pass up a chance to dissect a real-life one. It was an activity that got very lively at times, and it had earned them odd glances from eavesdroppers when they were out to dinner and having one of their discussions.

"We're not having an official meeting until tomorrow," Jessica reminded them. "So back to DeeDee's theory. The husband would have had to make sure the hired thugs beat him up enough that he wouldn't be suspected. But what if they got too enthusiastic and killed him by accident?"

Mary nodded. "It seems like it would be too risky."

"It's funny how people spin these stories," DeeDee remarked. "I don't know what Andy would do if a couple of guys tried to take Zoe and Polly and me. I'd like to think he'd give them a good pounding."

Kaylee had to laugh at the thought of DeeDee's mild-mannered husband giving anyone a good pounding. She laughed a little harder when one of the shop's patrons gave her a horrified look as she passed their table. She must be a visitor. Most people who frequented the café were used to the Petals and their quirky ways.

"On that happy note, I'm going to head over to the shop," Mary announced, picking up her bag.

Mary was the part-time floral designer at The Flower Patch, and Kaylee was quite certain she couldn't run the shop without Mary's assistance.

"I'll meet you over there in a few minutes," Kaylee said.

Mary waved and hurried out the side door.

The front door opened, and Jay Akin, the local funeral director's son, walked in, followed closely by two men Kaylee didn't recognize.

The older man wore a suit that Kaylee estimated cost about a month's worth of sales at The Flower Patch. The younger man, who was the spitting image of his companion, wore a slightly less expensive suit, but he had the same aloof demeanor.

By contrast, Jay wore slightly wrinkled black pants and a casual shirt. His red hair was disheveled, as if he'd been running his fingers through it repeatedly, and there were bags under his eyes.

Kaylee was surprised by Jay's haggard appearance. It was unusual to see him this way. She'd gotten to know him pretty well over the past few months, thanks to their early running schedules that coincided most mornings. They'd come to enjoy their quiet time in the park before the rest of Turtle Cove came to life.

On the mornings when Kaylee had gotten up but felt like she was dragging, Jay was the one with more energy, pushing her to do another half mile. Then again, he was fifteen years her junior, so she chalked up some of his seemingly boundless energy to that factor.

Kaylee waved at Jay, but he was focused on something the older man was saying, and he didn't seem to notice her.

Jessica leaned forward, eyebrows raised. "Who's that with Jay?" she asked, dropping her voice so they wouldn't hear. "He seems important." She tilted her head, regarding the stranger from different angles.

DeeDee glanced over at the men. "No idea."

Kaylee studied the man. His posture exuded authority, and he commanded attention. She couldn't help but notice that he was in charge of the conversation. His strong voice carried throughout the café, though she couldn't hear his exact words. She wondered what he was saying to Jay.

The younger stranger seemed detached from the conversation. He stared intently at something on his phone while the conversation swirled around him.

Jay seemed unsure what to do with his hands, moving them from his pockets to crossing them over his chest, then back again. He nodded while the older man continued speaking to him.

"Oh!" Kaylee said. "Jay told me the other morning that Giles Akin is hosting a convention for funeral directors, and the opening dinner is tonight. The man must be here for that. He definitely resembles a funeral director."

Jessica nodded. "The convention was a big topic at the last town meeting because the inn might not hold all the attendees. Giles was searching for an overflow location, and he wanted everyone to be prepared for an influx of business. Do you remember, DeeDee?"

"Of course I remember." DeeDee sniffed. "Giles and I planned an event at the bookshop during the convention." She shot Kaylee a teasing grin. "So what exactly does a funeral director look like?"

"You know what I mean," Kaylee said. "He has an air of seriousness, and he's wearing a suit."

"And a fancy suit at that. I guess death really does pay," Jessica commented, then stood. "I'm going to go take care of them."

DeeDee grinned. "You're just being nosy."

Jessica stuck her tongue out over her shoulder as she hurried behind the counter. "So what can I get you gentlemen this morning?" she asked brightly.

The two unfamiliar men stepped up to the counter, still reading the menu above Jessica's head.

"My son and I will have cappuccinos with almond milk," the older man said. "You do have alternate milks, don't you?"

"Absolutely," Jessica replied. "We have almond, soy, and coconut milk."

"Good. I hate it when little shops don't make considerations for people who don't meet their small-town stereotype," the man complained. "There are many people who don't drink cow's milk. We're just not meant to drink that. But there are a lot of closed-minded people on the subject who refuse to evolve with the times."

Kaylee and DeeDee glanced at each other. That sort of attitude wouldn't go over well with Jessica. A little shop? Closed-minded? And why was he so riled up about dairy products? Even before Jessica responded, Kaylee knew her friend was bristling.

Jessica paused, her fingers hovering over the cash register. "For a *little shop*, we're quite attuned with what people need and want in this day and age," she said. Her tone was still cheery to anyone who didn't know her well, but Kaylee could hear the contempt dripping through the words.

Kaylee turned slightly in her chair to get a better view of this train wreck.

"And I daresay that the people of this island are some of the most open-minded I've ever met," Jessica continued. She still smiled, but her dark eyes snapped.

Kaylee winced, sensing the storm that was about to be unleashed on their snobbish visitor. Maybe she should go help. She looked at her cup and saw that her latte was almost empty. Asking for a refill would be a good excuse to interrupt.

Jay stepped up to the counter, obviously sharing Kaylee's idea, and addressed Jessica. "Good morning. Can I get a double espresso, please?"

"Sure," Jessica said.

Kaylee walked up next to Jay, an extra reinforcement if needed between Jessica and the visitor. "I didn't know you were drinking coffee again," she said, giving Jay a hug. "We've missed our runs lately."

Jay stared down at his feet. "I know. I've been busy," he mumbled. "And tired. Hence the coffee."

"I get it," Kaylee said. "I hate it when real life interrupts good intentions."

A few weeks ago, Jay had told her that he was trying to get healthier. He planned to cut out red meat and caffeine from his diet and eat more vegetables. In addition, he was going to start lifting weights because he wanted to shed his thin frame and develop more muscle.

Kaylee figured he had his sights set on a potential girlfriend and was trying to up his game. Jay had admitted that he didn't have the easiest time talking to women.

But lately Jay hadn't been in the park, likely because he'd been working extra hours at the funeral parlor. His father, Giles, wanted him to be ready to take over the business in ten years or so. Maybe he'd handed the reins of this big event over to his son.

Jessica shifted her attention to Jay. "So who are your friends?" she asked as she began filling their orders.

"Mitchum Landsdowne," Jay said. "He's in town for the convention. And this is Christopher, his son."

Christopher Landsdowne glanced up from his phone and nodded before returning his attention to his device.

"Apparently, Jay has forgotten my name," Jessica broke in. "I'm Jessica Roberts, owner of this café and proud saleswoman of many alternative milks."

Mitchum smiled at Jessica, displaying sparkling white teeth. "It's wonderful to meet you," he said, taking her hand and bringing it to his lips. "You have a lovely café in a lovely town. I remember seeing this place before when I've been here on business, but regrettably I never made it inside. I have a feeling it could become addictive." He winked at her. "Especially taking the almond milk into consideration."

"Thank you," Jessica said, then gestured to Kaylee. "This is Kaylee Bleu. She owns the flower shop next door."

Mitchum turned to Kaylee. "I'm pleased to meet you too."

Kaylee tried not to wrinkle her nose. He sounded like a shyster. She wasn't in the habit of judging people on the first meeting, but something about him set her teeth on edge. "Welcome to Turtle Cove," she said, shaking his hand.

"You run a flower shop, then?" Mitchum motioned to Jessica's prized geranium, Oliver, that sat proudly on the counter. "Maybe you can help Ms. Roberts with her plant. He's looking sad."

Jessica gazed at Oliver.

Kaylee knew her friend got very worried when Oliver drooped. "He's just a little thirsty," she suggested, then steered the conversation back to Mitchum. "I hope your convention goes well."

"I'm sure it will," Mitchum said, adjusting his glasses. "Despite what people think, we funeral directors have many interesting things to talk about." He opened his wallet, removed a few bills, and dropped them into the tip jar.

"We love it when our little island gets visitors," Jessica said. She'd apparently forgiven Mitchum's initial comments about his milk preferences, because her tone was friendly. "It really makes us happy to be able to show off how great this town is. And as business owners, we love the extra sales."

"I'll bet," Mitchum said. "It's a wonderful opportunity for everyone. All the funeral directors are quite happy to be here." Then he said to Jay in a completely different, rather high-handed tone, "Are you getting our coffees?"

"Yes sir," Jay answered.

Kaylee caught the sarcasm in his tone, but Mitchum didn't seem to. He nodded at Jessica, then walked to the table in the far corner to wait for his minion to bring the order over.

Christopher followed his father. Kaylee wondered how he didn't bump into something, since he didn't glance up from his phone once.

Jessica raised her eyebrows and stared at Kaylee, who shrugged.

Kaylee turned to Jay. "So no runs for a few days?"

Jay sighed. "Not until the convention's over. I doubt I'll have the time or the energy to fit any in."

"Is everything okay?" she asked softly.

"What? Oh yeah. Sure," Jay said, glancing anxiously over his shoulder to where Mitchum checked his watch and his phone at the same time.

"He seems . . . challenging," Kaylee prompted.

Jay shrugged. "He's a big name in the biz," he said as if that explained everything.

"What do you mean?"

"He owns the Landsdowne Funeral Homes," Jay replied. "They've been expanding all over the state. Mitchum and his team have a good deal of influence. My dad is taking this convention very seriously, and he's paranoid about impressing Mitchum." He frowned. "Dad's making me entertain him."

"Why is Mitchum acting like you're his waiter?" Kaylee asked.

Jay reddened, then turned to Jessica. "Are those coffees ready?"

"Coming right up." She set the three cups on the counter.

Jay paid Jessica for the drinks, and she handed him the change.

Once Jay had the coffees in hand, he went over to the table where Mitchum and Christopher waited.

Mitchum tapped his foot, obviously impatient and doing his best to show Jay that the delay was hardly acceptable.

Kaylee got a coffee to go and returned to the table. She sat down next to DeeDee.

Her friend scrolled through something on her phone. "See," she said triumphantly, waving her phone around. "There's a whole comment thread that agrees with me."

"What are you talking about?" Kaylee asked, distracted by what was going on at Jay's table.

"A comment thread about the murder mystery I just read," DeeDee said. "A ton of people are saying the same things I did. The husband had to be in on it." She poked Kaylee. "Hey, you're not listening."

Kaylee faced DeeDee. "Oh. Sorry."

"What's going on over there?" DeeDee peered over at the corner where Jay and his companions were having a serious conversation.

Rather, Mitchum was having a serious conversation. Jay nodded, and every now and then he tried to get a word in edgewise, but it didn't seem to be working. Christopher was still preoccupied with his phone and didn't appear to be listening at all.

"I have no idea," Kaylee said.

Jessica returned to the table and slid into her seat. "Mitchum Landsdowne is kind of big for his britches," she commented. "I wonder if Giles is paying Jay overtime to take that abuse."

"I know. I feel terrible for Jay," Kaylee said. "But you seemed to forgive Mitchum pretty fast."

Jessica shrugged. "He made Jay pay, but he left a nice tip in the jar."

"He also insulted Oliver," Kaylee reminded her.

"True," Jessica conceded. "I hope it's not a bad sign that Oliver was droopy today. I gave him some of his favorite plant food."

"I'm sure he'll be fine," DeeDee reassured her.

"I need to go," Kaylee said. "I can't leave Mary alone to fend for herself. We've got a few orders, and tourist season will be starting soon." She took the last bite of her croissant and slung her bag over her shoulder.

"Call me later," Jessica said. "We need an agenda for our meeting tomorrow."

"I'll be sure to—" Kaylee stopped at the sound of Mitchum's angry voice reverberating through the café.

"I don't care about any of that," Mitchum snapped. His voice was low, but this time the words carried. "You owe me an answer."

Jay didn't say anything. He simply rose and shoved his chair aside, then stalked across the room and out the door.

2

Mitchum stared after Jay, then got up and followed, his expensive Italian shoes slapping against the floor.

Christopher, apparently just noticing he'd been left behind, rose with a sigh, picked up his to-go cup, and left the shop too.

Kaylee, DeeDee, and Jessica all gaped at one another.

"This is definitely going to be a long week for Jay," Kaylee said. "What do you think they were arguing about?"

DeeDee shrugged. "Maybe which crematory is the best one to use. Or who writes the most comprehensive obituaries," she suggested with a twinkle in her eyes. "Why are we so obsessed with these guys?"

Jessica smiled. "New blood. It's always interesting when visitors are in town. Not to mention, I'm totally intrigued by the funeral home business."

"You are?" DeeDee asked. "Since when?"

"Since always," Jessica said. "Giles has so many great stories when he stops in for coffee. Now that I think about it, I'm kind of surprised I haven't heard more hype about the convention."

"Me too," Kaylee admitted. "It seems odd. Everyone usually loves it when guests come to town."

"It doesn't look like Jay loves the guests," Jessica said. "Or at least not Mitchum Landsdowne."

"I'd better go." Kaylee raised an eyebrow at her friends. "Try not to get into trouble, all right?"

Jessica grinned. "Trouble? Us? I'm insulted."

Chuckling, Kaylee headed next door to The Flower Patch. She took a second to admire the Victorian mansion that housed her flower shop. It painted a lovely picture against the spring backdrop. The Flower Patch sign hung above the lovely wrap-around porch, gold leaf spelling out the name against a deep green background. Baskets of hanging flowers, white wooden rockers, and wicker tables contributed to the homey feeling she had worked hard to cultivate.

As expected, Mary's car was in the parking lot. Unexpected, however, was Reese's black pickup. She couldn't help the smile that broke out on her face or the accelerated pounding of her heart. "Stop it," she said out loud. "I'm sure he's only here to pick something up or maybe to fix the window that won't shut right."

Kaylee was grateful for his help. Reese stopped by regularly to see if she needed something fixed. Deep down, she hoped it had less to do with obligation and more to do with liking her company.

She stepped inside. Bear was basking in the glow of the morning sun through the windows. His little paws rested on either side of his striped bow tie.

Kaylee crouched to scratch his ears. "How are you doing, Bear Dog?" she asked. "You ready for work?"

Bear sighed.

Kaylee laughed. "I feel the same way. I'm ready to go back to bed."

"Do you need a nap while you wait for your coffee to kick in?" Mary asked from the counter.

"No, I'll be fine. Bear can nap for both of us." He even had a bed in her second-floor office in case the main floor got too busy. There were some days she wanted to curl up on the pillow with him or on one of the couches in the consultation area, but she had to maintain a modicum of dignity if she wanted to make sure her customers would return.

"You're lucky to be right next door to the bakery. You can run over for more coffee whenever you need it." Reese leaned against the counter with a broad smile on his handsome face.

"I take advantage of that far too often," she told him.

Mary was arranging a vase of gorgeous *Hemerocallis*. The daylilies were bright shades of yellow and gold, with touches of maroon here and there and just the right amount of greenery. She set her scissors down. "I think that does it," she said.

Bear yipped.

"Your input on my designs is invaluable, Bear," Mary said with a smile.

Reese scratched behind Bear's ears, then handed Kaylee a travel mug filled with a thick green liquid. "I'm testing a new smoothie recipe, and I wanted you to try it and tell me what you think."

Kaylee grinned and accepted the drink. "How did you know I needed something healthy to balance out the coffee and chocolate I've had this morning? Did Mary tattle on me?"

Mary laughed. "I don't think Reese needs me to tell him how often we're at Jess's. He's a pretty smart guy. Besides, he already had that when he showed up."

"Good point." Kaylee laughed too.

Mary squeezed Kaylee's arm. "I'll get started on some of our other orders. And this needs a ribbon." She picked up the scissors and vase and retreated to the workroom.

Kaylee turned her attention back to Reese. "I didn't know you made smoothies," she said, taking a sip.

"They're my specialty. I'm a bachelor after all. What do you think?"

It was creamy and fruity and the perfect shade of green to convince her it was healthy. "It's delicious."

Reese grinned. "I'm glad you like it. I have another one

in the cooler in my truck. I think it'll make a nice midmorning pick-me-up." His phone rang, and he glanced at the screen. "Just a second."

She stashed her purse behind the counter and checked their orders list while he had a brief conversation. After he hung up, she gave him a questioning look.

"I have an emergency at Northern Lights," he explained with a sigh. "It's Monday morning, so there has to be an emergency, right?"

"Right," Kaylee replied. The Northern Lights Inn was one of the best places to stay in Turtle Cove, and this week it was full of Giles's funeral director friends. "What's going on?"

"There's a leak in one of the rooms. Of course, they're completely booked and can't move the guest to another room. They don't want to have to send anyone to a different hotel, so I need to figure it out fast."

"I'm sorry. Maybe dinner after work would help? That is, if your emergency gets solved."

Reese smiled. "How about O'Brien's at eight?"

"That sounds great," she said. O'Brien's seafood was always a treat, and Bear could join them because the restaurant featured a dog-friendly patio. She hated leaving him home alone.

"What's on your schedule for the day?" Reese asked.

"I'm planning to design some new bouquets for weddings and showers. It'll be nice to lie low and be creative. Hopefully there will be no floral emergencies," she added with a grin.

"That sounds like a good start to the week." Reese checked his watch. "I'd better head out. Should I pick you up at home or—"

He was cut off when the doorbell jingled. Giles Akin burst into the shop, followed by Nathan Anghelone and his wife, Abby.

Giles seemed flustered, which was odd for the island coroner and funeral home director. Given his line of work,

Giles was normally calm, cool, and collected. But today he wasn't wearing a suit jacket, his tie was askew, and his brown hair was mussed.

Kaylee wondered if whatever was bothering him had anything to do with Jay and Mitchum's apparent fight. But why would Giles be coming to tell her about it?

Nathan appeared more relaxed. He was about ten years younger than Giles, and he owned a funeral home in nearby Eastsound. Nathan had carefully styled jet-black hair, and he wore jeans and a casual button-down shirt. He looked more like someone who had stepped off the page of a fashion magazine than a funeral director. Kaylee assumed that Nathan was more composed than Giles because he was probably assisting Giles this week and not actually running the convention.

Abby acted downright delighted. She rushed over to the cooler and pressed her face against it. "Oh my goodness, those tulips!" she squealed. "How gorgeous! Nathan, come and see. The kids would love them."

Nathan walked over to stand next to his wife, nodding as she pointed out the various flowers.

"Kaylee, I need your help," Giles said, breathless. Then he seemed to remember his manners. "I'm sorry to interrupt, but I have a small emergency."

Reese chuckled. "That seems to be the theme of the day." He grinned at Kaylee. "I'll be in touch about tonight." With a nod, he walked out.

Kaylee focused her attention on Giles. "What's going on?" she asked. "Is everything all right?"

Giles grimaced. "Not really. I'm afraid my party-planning skills are sorely lacking. We're having our funeral directors' convention here in town this week, as you know."

Kaylee nodded. "I saw Jay this morning with Mitchum

Landsdowne and his son."

"You did?" Giles asked, frowning. "Where?"

"At the bakery."

Giles looked like he was about to say something but decided against it. "Tonight is our kickoff dinner at the park. I hired a caterer and rented the tent, the tables, and even the table linens. Enough for thirty people. I thought I'd taken care of everything."

"That sounds great," Kaylee said.

Giles sighed. "The trouble is, it's missing something. When I called Thelma over to get her opinion, she couldn't believe what I forgot."

Kaylee knew that Thelma, Giles's wife, would have a good perspective on whatever it was. "Well, don't keep me on the edge of my seat. What did you forget?" But she had a sinking feeling she already knew.

"Flowers," Nathan supplied from across the room, where he was rubbing Bear's belly.

Giles nodded sadly. "Yes, and lots of them."

Kaylee stifled a groan, watching her relaxed Monday evaporate before her eyes. "How many arrangements do you need?"

"We have six tables for the dinner, and we'd also like some arrangements on the food tables, as well as some standing arrangements to be scattered around the tent," Giles said, his expression reminding her of Bear's when he'd done something wrong.

"I don't mean any disrespect," Kaylee said, "but you handle funerals with lots of flowers. How did you forget the flowers?"

Giles hung his head, dejected. "There have been so many details to this week that flowers must have simply slipped through the cracks. I'm sorry to put so much pressure on you."

Nathan started strolling around the room again but not before Kaylee saw him smile at his friend's discomfort.

"Let's have a seat and figure out exactly what you need,"

Kaylee said, leading Giles over to the sitting area that she used for consultations. She motioned to a chair.

"You can do it?" Giles asked, his relief apparent.

Kaylee gave him a smile. The man didn't need to feel guiltier than he already did. "It won't be easy, but yes, we can do it."

"Thank you," Giles said, taking a seat. "You're a godsend. Truly."

"I don't know about that," Kaylee said, pulling out the binder of arrangement examples she used for events. She sat down next to him. "What's the overall theme of the dinner? What's the mood you're hoping to achieve?"

Giles widened his eyes. He appeared panicked again.

Kaylee suppressed a smile. Giles could put together the most tasteful and beautiful way to see someone off to the afterlife, but he couldn't figure out how to plan a dinner for a group of living people.

"I don't know," Giles said. He glanced at Nathan. "Formal, I guess."

Nathan shrugged as if to say, *How should I know?*

"It's all right. We'll find something." Kaylee opened the binder and flipped through the pages. "How about one of these?" She pointed out a few pictures.

Giles was silent as he studied them.

"We could do dahlias," Kaylee suggested. "We have them in a number of colors. I could add other flowers to make the arrangements more interesting, but dahlias would be your main draw."

Nathan joined them and peered over Kaylee's shoulder. "Those look fine to me. What do you think, Abby?" He waved his wife over.

She left the fresh blooms to come and study the book. "They're absolutely lovely. I think they'd be perfect. Don't you, Giles?"

"Lovely. Perfect," Giles echoed. "How fast can you get the

arrangements done and delivered? Our cocktail hour begins at seven."

Kaylee cringed inwardly, picturing all the work ahead of her and Mary to pull this order off on such short notice. Once again, she thought longingly of her original plan to spend the day taking it easy, putting a few arrangements together, and sketching out some new ideas.

But duty called, and she was never one to shirk it.

Besides, she liked Giles and wanted his event to be a success.

Not to mention, Kaylee knew what it was like to miss an important detail. Before moving to Turtle Cove, Kaylee had been a plant taxonomy professor at the University of Washington in Seattle and occasionally served as a forensic botanist for the Seattle police. She had understood that life and known all the ins and outs. But when her position at the university was eliminated and she'd bought The Flower Patch from her grandmother, Kaylee had been completely lost. She'd frequently missed or forgotten orders. She was lucky that Mary had been there to back her up and keep things on track.

Kaylee smiled brightly at Giles. "Let's go over to the park and check out the setup. In the meantime, I'll ask Mary to start putting some of the table centerpieces together. Are the tables round?"

Nathan nodded.

As if sensing that she was needed, Mary came out of the workroom and joined them in the consultation area. She greeted Giles, Nathan, and Abby.

"Can you start on some centerpieces for Giles's event tonight?" Kaylee asked.

"Sure thing," Mary answered. "What kind of event is it?"

"An outdoor dinner in a tent." Kaylee pointed to the arrangement they'd settled on. "Something along these lines, for round tables. I'm going over to the park with Giles to get a better sense of the setup."

Mary nodded. "You got it." She smiled at them and patted Giles's shoulder. "Don't worry. We'll make sure it's a night everyone will remember."

3

"This will be amazing," Kaylee told Giles. "I promise."

Kaylee had followed Giles to the park, and now they were checking out the site for the dinner. Giles had picked a gorgeous spot overlooking the water. The event was going to be beautiful, especially given the mild, sunny weather. Spring on Orcas Island was one of the best times of the year. It wasn't hot yet, and tourists weren't thronging the streets and the beaches.

Not that Kaylee didn't love tourists, who frequented her store as much as the locals. Caught up in the romance of a vacation, many tourists bought flowers for their significant others, which usually resulted in a secondary sale of a pretty vase, because who brought a vase on vacation?

The general area had been cordoned off for the event already, and the tent was set up. The trees surrounding it had been strung with lights, courtesy of the parks and recreation department. It was obvious that the employees enjoyed showing off the island's natural beauty.

Nathan and Abby pulled up and got out of the car, then walked over to them.

"Sorry we're late," Nathan said. "I had to make a call."

"We haven't been here long," Giles said. "Let's take a peek inside the tent."

They filed inside.

"Who's doing the rest of the decorating?" Kaylee asked, glancing around the practically empty tent. Only the dining and food tables were set up, and there was nothing on them. Not even tablecloths.

Nathan laughed. "I don't think we're doing much else. The caterers are bringing tablecloths and such, but we didn't think further ahead than that."

"Next year you need to get a real party planner involved," Abby said.

"What do you mean, next year?" Giles asked in mock horror. "I'm not planning on hosting this convention for another ten years. There are plenty of other people it can circulate through before coming back to me." He sighed. "But I should have brought Thelma in much sooner. It's definitely not my area of expertise."

"So you're not putting tiny coffins and hearses on every table?" Kaylee teased, trying to make Giles feel better.

"Oh no," Giles said, clearly appalled. "This crowd doesn't go for cutesy things like that. I envisioned a simple night with good food and good weather." He smiled. "At least I remembered to order the food."

Kaylee retrieved a notebook and a pencil from her bag and walked around the tent, jotting down notes and making sketches of where the floral arrangements should be positioned. Then she took photos of the area and sent them to Mary to give her a better idea of the setup.

"It's all going to work out perfectly," Abby announced as she gazed around the tent. "The weather is supposed to stay beautiful. Everyone's going to have a great time."

"Abby's right," Nathan said to Giles. "Stop worrying. Kaylee's got everything under control, and it's going to be a great kickoff to a great event. Okay?" He slung his arm around Giles's shoulder. "You worry too much."

"Thelma thinks flowers will pull the whole event together, and she's always right about such things," Giles replied.

"Flowers definitely make the event, but I've got you covered."

Kaylee gave Giles a thumbs-up. "I'm heading back to the shop to get started."

Giles nodded. "Jay is in charge of getting everything set up and ready to go. He'll be around later if you need him."

"Your party begins at seven, so I'll make sure everything's here by five." Kaylee checked her watch and grimaced. That was an awfully short deadline, but at least she'd sent Mary photos of the setup. She knew Mary would already be well into the arrangements by the time she got back to the shop.

On the way to the park, she'd called her new temporary deliveryman, Seamus McCreary, and asked him to be on standby. Fortunately, he was available. She was thankful that she'd taken a chance and hired him. She didn't particularly need a deliveryman at the moment, but he had asked for work, and she liked to help when she could. That generosity was about to pay off.

Giles's phone rang, and he glanced at the screen. "I'm afraid Mrs. Moriarty may have passed, which is going to take me away from the proceedings for a while."

"Let me know if there's anything Abby and I can do to help," Nathan offered.

Giles nodded, then faced Kaylee. "Thank you. We'll see you later on." When he answered the call, his voice was calm and compassionate.

Kaylee smiled. It was amazing to her that someone who was so comfortable with the deceased and bereaved could be as uncomfortable with the living as Giles clearly was about this party.

Giles walked away, and Nathan and Abby followed.

Kaylee regarded the tent one last time, making mental notes on how best to fill the space. "We have a busy day ahead of us," she murmured to herself.

She only hoped they would be able to accomplish everything on time.

On her way back to the shop, Kaylee mentally reviewed her to-do list. She hoped she had enough of each kind of flower to do the arrangements the way she wanted them. It would have been nice to know about this job in advance so she could have ensured she had enough flowers on hand. But there was nothing to be done about it now, and she would just have to make the best of it.

Besides, she had a feeling that Giles wouldn't be paying much attention to the actual flowers as long as there was something pretty sitting on the tables and everywhere else she'd sketched out inside the tent. He probably would have been happy with only centerpieces.

However, Kaylee never did things halfway. There would be flowers all around the tent in tall and short vases and even a couple of hanging arrangements. If she didn't have the flowers to create perfectly uniform arrangements, she could at least make them look intentional by ensuring they all fit the same theme. That was actually a fairly popular technique with decorations these days, and she'd noticed that it could really jazz up a room.

Feeling better with both a plan and a backup plan, she made a pit stop at the craft store for more wire and other things she knew they were low on, then pulled into the flower shop's parking lot.

Of course, on a day when they needed quiet, the store was packed with customers. The nice weather must have brought them out. Some people wanted to dress up their flower beds, and others wanted to get ideas for future events. A few were there to pick up bouquets for wives or girlfriends.

Kaylee jumped in to help Mary. Between the two of them, they cheerfully juggled their customers and worked on Giles's order. Kaylee figured that if push came to shove later, she could close the shop for the last few hours of the day to make sure they finished the party arrangements on time. She wanted to hold off as long as possible, though. She couldn't afford to give up sales as quickly as they were coming in today.

During one of the lulls, Bear settled down on the floor in the workroom for a nap. Apparently, all his socializing had worn him out.

"It's lucky we're both good at this," Mary said with a sigh as she finished the last of the table arrangements at what seemed like record speed.

Kaylee studied one of the hanging arrangements, which had become more complicated than she'd intended, and laughed. "I'm wondering right now if I really am any good. This isn't doing what I want it to." She tugged a wire.

"Let me see." Mary assessed the project from all sides, then sat down on a stool and began undoing some of Kaylee's painstaking work. "What about this?" She quickly moved a few stems and added several pieces of greenery.

Kaylee beamed. "You're a genius. Thank you. I was stressing out about it."

"I can see that." Mary smiled. She reached into the cabinet behind her to pull out some strips of lace. "These will finish it off nicely." She tied large bows around each container.

"Wonderful," Kaylee said as she regarded Mary's work. "It's exactly what I was going for."

Bear glanced up and yipped.

"You even have Bear's seal of approval." Kaylee smiled at Mary. "I'm so glad you're here. I couldn't do it without you."

"Thank you, hon." Mary put her hand over Kaylee's and

squeezed. "Now what else do we need for this shindig?"

Kaylee grabbed her notebook and flipped to her scribbled notes and rough diagram of the setup. She handed it to Mary. "What do you think?"

Mary perused the pages. "How about putting some of those pedestals out at the entrance with a few tall arrangements?"

"Yes, that sounds great." Kaylee checked her watch. They were cutting it closer than she normally liked to. She had told Giles the arrangements would be on-site by five, but her perfectionist side wouldn't let her send out anything that didn't meet her standards. "Do we have any of the pedestals, though? I thought we rented them all out to the Carlisles for the wedding rehearsal."

"We did, but they dropped them off the other day."

"Good," Kaylee said. "Do you think we have enough time?"

"I can work on them right now," Mary offered. "The centerpieces are done, and Seamus is on his way over to the park with them. I helped him pack them up. You seemed to be in the zone, and I didn't want to disturb you."

"Thank you." Kaylee took a breath. "Do you want to tackle those other arrangements together?"

"Let's do it."

Kaylee and Mary got back to work. The arrangements came together well, but it was nearly five o'clock when they put the finishing touches on the last bouquets. They were down to the wire.

"They're stunning," Kaylee said, stepping back to admire them.

"They really are," Mary agreed. "Do you want me to call Seamus to pick up these arrangements and the pedestals?"

Kaylee thought for a minute. "He already delivered the centerpieces, so let's not bother him again. I can take them. I have to set everything up anyway."

"I have a prior engagement tonight, but I can push it back if you need me to come and help."

"I wouldn't dream of making you rearrange your schedule. I'm the one who agreed to do this at the last minute." She smiled. "Go have a great time."

"Thanks. I will. Herb and I are going out to dinner with friends to celebrate their anniversary." Mary picked up an arrangement. "I can at least help you load the car."

"Thanks, but I can handle it."

Mary started for the door, then paused and turned to Kaylee. "Everything is gorgeous. You have such a talent. Your grandmother would be proud. I'll definitely tell her about this the next time I call her."

Kaylee felt her throat tighten at the unexpected compliment. Her grandma had moved to Arizona to live with her sister, and Kaylee missed her. "Thank you. That means a lot."

Mary smiled. "Well, it's true. Have a good night."

Kaylee watched her friend go. There was nothing she wanted more than her grandparents—she was certain Grandpa was watching over her and the shop from heaven—to be proud of her. To hear one of her grandmother's closest friends articulate that sentiment was amazing.

But she didn't have time to be lost in her emotions right now. If she didn't get the event set up, Mary would certainly have to rethink her compliment.

"Come on, Bear," she called. "We have to get this done."

Bear jumped up and beat her to the door.

Once the arrangements, the pedestals, and her little companion were loaded into the car, Kaylee headed to the park, her mind already skipping ahead to her evening with Reese. He was such a nice guy, and she was looking forward to spending time with him. They got along so well, and he seemed to feel the same way.

"Right, Bear?" she asked, glancing in the rearview mirror.

The dog snored softly in response.

"A lot of help you are," Kaylee said with a grin.

But Bear roused a few minutes later when she pulled into the park. He sat up and barked.

"Let's get this stuff dropped off so we can go home and I can get ready for dinner," Kaylee told him.

She scanned the area. The park was quiet. Parents had taken their children home for dinner, and it was off-hours for the business people who liked to stroll here during the day. She'd expected to see more activity for the party, though.

She wasn't surprised that the red Prius Seamus used to deliver flowers wasn't here. He had already come and gone. Jay's car and a catering van were parked on the far side of the lot.

It didn't seem like anyone else was around, which surprised her. She would have thought that at least the caterer would be on-site setting up. Cocktail hour was a little less than two hours away.

At least she could get her work done in peace. She opened the door and grabbed one of the arrangements out of the car, thankful that it hadn't toppled over during the drive.

Then she let Bear out of the car. But instead of staying near her feet as usual, he raced to the tent, barking up a storm.

"Bear!" Kaylee called. "Come back here!" She wondered why the dog was so worked up. He didn't normally act like this.

Bear ignored her.

Kaylee sighed as she followed him. The arrangement was heavy, and she had to walk slowly.

When she finally joined Bear at the entrance to the tent, he was barking so fiercely his whole body wagged.

After depositing the arrangement on the ground, she reached down and grabbed Bear's leash. "What's going on, buddy?"

Bear kept barking.

Kaylee scooped him up and stepped into the tent. At first, she saw nothing out of the ordinary. The table linens had arrived, and Seamus had set the flowers out on the tables. One of the arrangements was off-center. Kaylee went over to straighten it, noticing the linen wasn't completely even either.

Then she froze as she saw what Bear was so freaked out about.

There was a body on the ground. A man's body. He lay on his side, one hand stretched slightly forward, as if he'd been reaching for something. A pair of glasses lay broken near the body.

And if Kaylee didn't recognize his still, deathly pale face, all she needed to do was look at his feet.

The man wore the same expensive Italian shoes Mitchum Landsdowne had had on this morning.

4

Kaylee couldn't move for a full minute.

When her brain finally started to work again, she inched closer to the body, gazing at the man's feet. It seemed easier to focus on his expensive Italian shoes instead of his face. At the same time, she tried to soothe Bear, who was now barking so frantically that she felt like her eardrum was about to shatter.

She paused, dread swelling up in her stomach, bile rising in her throat. Her initial assessment of the shoes had been right. There was no mistaking who it was.

Mitchum Landsdowne. Jay's coffee date, the man who'd caused Jay to storm out of the café this morning. The man who'd been able to insult Jessica and then buy his way back into her good graces with a generous tip.

Kaylee crept closer, her instincts telling her to check for a pulse, even though she knew it was useless. But then what?

No. Don't touch him. I might contaminate something.

Instead, she forced herself to stop and examine her surroundings.

Other than the body, so oddly out of place in this scene, the tent was as she'd left it mere hours earlier, with more of the party aspects in place. The bar had been delivered, and the heating trays for the pans of food were set out on the tables. A separate table held a punch bowl with red liquid in it and some ice cubes floating on the top. It seemed too early to put the punch out, but maybe it was for the caterers to drink as they set up.

The linens and centerpieces were perfectly arranged on the dinner tables. All except for the table next to Mitchum. It was the one that had led her over here in the first place, with the centerpiece askew, the tablecloth hanging lower on one side. He'd probably grabbed it when he fell.

Her instinct was to straighten the tablecloth, but then she realized not touching anything extended to the entire scene, not just the body. She had to talk to the sheriff's department, and the first thing they'd ask was if she touched something.

No, it would be better to wait for them and an ambulance. There was nothing she could do for Mitchum now anyway.

Kaylee backed out of the tent, shaking so hard she was afraid of dropping her dog. In her peripheral vision, she could see a few people wandering around the outer edges of the park. She had to get help before the dinner guests started arriving.

She set Bear on the ground, holding him firmly between her feet so he couldn't run in and disturb the scene. She should probably put him in the car, but the only thing worse than facing this situation with him would be trying to face it alone. She fished her cell phone out of her pocket. After hitting the wrong passcode twice, she finally gave up and used the emergency call button on the lock screen.

"911. What is your emergency?"

"I have . . . There's a—" Kaylee stopped and cleared her throat when she realized she was barely speaking above a whisper.

"Hello?" The dispatcher's tone became urgent. "Ma'am, what is the emergency?"

"I'm at the public park in Turtle Cove, and there's a body at the site of tonight's dinner party," she said, using all her effort to get the words out. "Please come. There are people around."

She answered the dispatcher's questions automatically. "My name is Kaylee Bleu . . . No, I don't know how he died. I just found him . . . Yes, I can stay on the line until someone gets here."

"You're doing great, ma'am," the dispatcher said kindly. "I

have to ask an unpleasant favor now."

"What is it?"

"I need you to go stand in the doorway to the tent and prevent anyone else from going in. The fewer people we have going through the crime scene, the easier it will be for the sheriff to figure out what happened."

Kaylee couldn't argue with that. She moved to the doorway as requested.

A man approached, carting a case of wine.

"You can't go in there," Kaylee said, holding up a hand in front of him.

"Excuse me?" The man gave her a withering stare. "Who are you?" he demanded as he tried to brush by her.

Bear barked at him.

"Would you call off your dog?" the bartender snapped. "I have a job to do."

"No, you can't go in," she said, holding her ground.

"Are you kidding me, lady?" he asked in disbelief.

Kaylee shook her head. "I'm sorry."

"You *will* be sorry when I tell the guy who hired me that you're holding things up." He stalked away in a huff, pulling out his cell phone.

She assumed he was going to call Giles and tell him some crazy woman with a dachshund wouldn't let him in the tent to finish setting up.

Kaylee sat on the ground near the entrance to the tent, and Bear curled up in her lap.

"Are you still there, Ms. Bleu?" the dispatcher asked, making her jump. She'd forgotten about the phone in her hand.

"Yes. Sorry. I think I'm in shock."

"Well, anyone would be."

As Kaylee watched the bartender pace, jabbing his finger in the air while he spoke—shouted, really—into his phone, it occurred to her how odd it was that Giles and Nathan hadn't arrived yet. The cocktail hour was supposed to start soon. And with the way they'd been fussing around earlier today, she'd expected them to be here overseeing Jay and making sure everything had arrived on time and looked good.

But Jay was nowhere in sight either, despite his car being in the parking lot. Perhaps Mrs. Moriarty's arrangements were taking longer than expected.

She heard the wail of sirens in the distance, getting closer. In a typical case like this, Giles would be on his way to the scene or the hospital as the coroner. But Mitchum was an attendee of Giles's convention. Would Giles still act as coroner?

"They're here," she said into the phone.

"Okay, I'll let you go then. Everything will be fine, Ms. Bleu." The dispatcher clicked off.

Kaylee almost swooned with relief when Sheriff Eddie Maddox drove up in his cruiser.

Maddox parked near the tent and right on the grass, which no doubt would cause the parks and recreation people some heartache. They took a lot of pride in their landscaping. But Kaylee imagined they wouldn't want to argue with the sheriff or get in the way of his investigation. The lights remained flashing as he climbed out of the car and strode over to Kaylee.

Deputy Nick Durham was with the sheriff. Nick exited the passenger side and waved encouragingly to Kaylee, then escorted the testy bartender away from the area. Kaylee noticed that the bartender's demeanor changed dramatically once the police arrived.

Maddox knelt down next to Kaylee. "What happened? Are you hurt?"

Bear wriggled in her arms. Kaylee knew she should put the

dog in the car, but right now she wanted to hold on to him. "I'm fine. But he's not," she said, motioning toward the tent behind her.

"Who's 'he'?" Maddox's voice was tense. "Did you recognize the victim?"

Kaylee nodded and tried to still her shaking hands. "His name is Mitchum Landsdowne. I met him this morning at the bakery. He was one of the funeral directors here for the convention."

Maddox let out a deep breath. "Go wait by my car. I'll be there in a moment."

Kaylee didn't move right away. Instead, she watched the sheriff carefully approach the tent.

Maddox glanced at the loose ropes that would hold back the part of the tent that could be used as a door if the weather was bad. Then he pulled out his cell phone and took pictures of the entrance to the tent, the flower arrangement Kaylee had left on the ground, and the grass leading inside the tent that she had probably flattened with her footsteps.

She turned her head as he crouched down next to where Mitchum lay.

Kaylee swallowed hard against the lump in her throat and hugged Bear tighter as she forced herself to stand. It wasn't chilly yet, but suddenly she felt cold from deep inside her bones. She staggered over to Maddox's cruiser and slumped against it, feeling like she was in a fog.

More sirens screamed as the ambulance pulled up as close as possible to the tent. The sirens cut abruptly, but the lights continued to flash as the EMTs hopped out and unloaded a stretcher from the back of the van.

A crowd had started to gather, obviously drawn by the lights and the police presence, and Nick directed the onlookers away from the area.

After the EMTs wheeled the stretcher inside the tent, Nick

stood guard at the entrance with his "don't mess with me" expression firmly in place.

A car pulling up behind the cruiser caught her attention. Kaylee sighed when she saw Giles jumping out of the passenger side almost before the vehicle stopped. As soon as Nathan parked the car, he leaped out too. Abby exited the back seat.

Giles rushed over to Kaylee. "What's going on?" The panic came through his voice loud and clear.

Kaylee stepped forward to prevent him from trying to get to the tent. "I'm so sorry. There's been a . . . mishap."

"A mishap? What kind of mishap?" Giles peered over her shoulder, trying to see what was going on. "I got a message from Kurt, the bartender. He sounded upset. What's happened?"

"Sheriff Maddox will be right over. It'll be better if he tells you." She blew out a breath and glanced at Giles's companions.

Nathan's face paled as he took in the scene and apparently started to put two and two together. Abby appeared frightened as she turned to her husband and gripped his hand.

"Is someone injured?" Giles asked Kaylee. "Did someone wander into our tent and get hurt? Where's Jay? Is he okay?"

"I haven't seen Jay," Kaylee said.

Maddox walked over and greeted the newcomers. "Giles, is this your party?"

"It was supposed to be," Giles said. "What's going on?"

"Let's talk over here," Maddox said, glancing at Kaylee, then leading them away.

She blew out a breath of frustration. After all, she was the one who'd found the body. It wasn't like Maddox was protecting her from anything.

Kaylee glanced over at Nick.

He met her gaze, his own expression unreadable.

She hugged Bear again. He'd calmed down since they'd moved

farther away from the tent, but he was still on alert. She watched Maddox talk and wondered what was going to happen next.

Her ringing phone jolted her out of her thoughts. She fished it out of her pocket and checked the screen. It was Mary. Taking a deep breath, she answered.

"I wanted to check and make sure everything's okay over there," Mary said.

"What do you mean?" Kaylee asked sharply.

"With the flowers." Mary sounded puzzled.

"Oh. Yes. Of course. I'm sorry." She sighed. "The flowers are fine, but I think the party is canceled."

"Canceled?" Mary repeated. "My goodness, why?"

Maddox's little circle dispersed.

"I'll explain later," Kaylee said. "Can I call you back?"

"Okay," her friend said, still sounding bewildered.

Still holding Bear, Kaylee hung up and headed toward the group.

Nathan seemed like he wasn't sure what to do. He and Abby wandered toward their car and sat in it, but they didn't drive away.

Giles went straight for the tent and disappeared inside, Maddox on his heels.

Kaylee considered trying to follow them inside, but she knew from experience that she wouldn't be able to get past Nick. He took his job seriously, and nothing got in the way of his police work.

She admired his dedication, but today she wished he'd let his gaurd down a little. She wanted to know what had happened to Mitchum, who had seemed so full of life this morning. He'd been self-assured, arrogant, and definitely at odds with Jay for whatever reason. He hadn't been a pleasant person, but the loss of life was tragic no matter who it was.

She wondered what Jay and Mitchum had been arguing about. Had Mitchum been stressed about something and given himself a heart attack? Or maybe it had been an aneurysm.

Kaylee shivered. She recalled stories of unsuspecting people going about their lives when suddenly they were killed by something they hadn't even realized was wreaking havoc on their bodies.

When something like that happened, she wanted to know why. It was almost like preparing herself. If she knew about all the things that could potentially harm her, maybe she could take an extra precaution or two.

She changed her mind about trying to get inside. "Hey," she said, stopping in front of Nick. "Anything I can do to help?"

"I don't think so."

"I figured Sheriff Maddox would want to talk to me since I found him and all," she pressed.

"Yeah, I'm sure he'll want to talk to you." He paused. "When he's done."

Kaylee didn't move.

Finally, Nick sighed. "Wait here." He disappeared inside the tent, returning a moment later with Maddox.

"I was coming to get you in a minute," Maddox told her. "I want you to walk me through what you saw when you got here. We can go sit in my car if you'd like."

Kaylee shook her head. "I'd rather stay outside. I could use the fresh air." She couldn't help but glance at the tent. She could see Giles standing near his colleague's prone body.

What could possibly have happened to Mitchum?

5

Sheriff Maddox motioned Kaylee toward one of the picnic tables. "Let's talk over there."

Kaylee slid onto a bench. She put Bear at her feet and scanned the breathtaking view of the water. Gazing at the water normally soothed her, but right now it did nothing to calm her.

Maddox sat on the opposite bench and studied her. "Please walk me through what happened today."

Kaylee paused as she gathered her thoughts. "This morning Giles and Nathan came by the shop because they realized they'd forgotten to order flowers for the dinner party."

The sheriff pulled a notepad and a pen out of his pocket and began taking notes. "So you agreed to provide the flowers."

"Yes. Mary and I spent the day putting arrangements together for them."

"Did you deliver the flowers yourself?" he asked.

"Our temporary delivery guy brought the centerpieces over earlier," Kaylee answered, "but I came over with the last of the arrangements and the pedestals. I had to set everything up anyway."

"What's his name?" Maddox asked, pen poised over his notepad.

"Seamus McCreary."

The sheriff cocked his head. "Is he from around here?"

"No, he's visiting family for the summer and wanted to make some money," Kaylee answered. "I told him I'd call him when I had deliveries and was too busy to get to them."

Maddox jotted down more notes. "What happened when

you arrived at the park?"

"Bear ran to the tent and started barking." She glanced down at her little dog, who'd flopped onto the grass, seemingly exhausted from his ordeal. "I went inside and saw Mitchum on the ground. What happened to him?"

"There's no way to know yet," the sheriff said, but something in his tone set Kaylee on edge. "We need to do an autopsy. So back to what you saw. Was anyone around?"

"The bartender. I think the caterers were on-site, but they must have been in the van."

"Is that the bartender?" Maddox pointed to the surly guy Kaylee had blocked from the tent. Nick must have told him to stay put, because he sat next to his case of wine.

Kaylee nodded. "That's him. Giles said his name is Kurt."

The sheriff wrote it down. "Do you know if he had been inside the tent?"

"I assume he was. There's a bowl of punch or something already set out, and the temporary bar is in there. The food tables were set up too, but there was no food yet."

"What about Jay?"

"I didn't see him, but I noticed his car parked in the lot."

"Was there anyone else around?" Maddox asked.

"Not that I saw. Will Giles still be the coroner?" Kaylee asked.

Maddox looked at her curiously. "Why wouldn't he?"

"I don't know. I thought it might be an issue since Giles knew Mitchum and Mitchum died at Giles's party."

"Did you know Mitchum?" Maddox asked.

"I met him this morning at Death by Chocolate. He was in there with Jay and his son, Christopher. He seemed like a pretty unpleasant person. I think he argued with Jay, and Jay left." Kaylee hated how that sounded for her friend, but she had to tell the truth.

Maddox made a note, then sat silently, drumming his fingers on the table. He scanned the park, and Kaylee couldn't tell if he was searching for someone or if he was processing his thoughts. "Okay," he said finally. "Thanks. If I have any other questions, I'll be in touch."

Kaylee rose to leave, holding on to the picnic table for a minute when her legs seemed to take a moment to work.

The sheriff studied her. "Do you need a ride?"

"No. I have my car." Hopefully she could drive it. Kaylee noticed Giles emerge from the tent. He stood off to the side, hands in his pockets, staring into the distance. "Can I go talk to Giles for a minute?"

Maddox narrowed his eyes. "Sure, but he's not going to tell you anything more."

That was an unexpected reaction. Kaylee lifted her chin, defiant. "I want to see if he's okay and if he needs help canceling the party before other people show up," she said, meeting his eyes levelly. "Come on, Bear."

As Kaylee and Bear walked over to Giles, her thoughts raced. Maddox's response to her question about how Mitchum died had been guarded at best. She'd expected him to tell her it was probably a heart attack. A case of another middle-aged man eating too much red meat or drinking too much alcohol.

But the sheriff had been almost defensive about the question, and he clearly didn't want her conversing about it with Giles. Not to mention all the questions he had about the scene and who was around. And why she'd been here.

Maybe Maddox thought foul play might be involved. That had to be the reason. Unless the sheriff was simply playing it safe.

The crowd of onlookers had grown after the arrival of the ambulance, and Nick was obviously on guard for anyone trying to breach his system and get closer to the action. He eyed Kaylee as she came closer.

She ignored him and went up to Giles. "Are you all right?" she asked softly.

He focused on her, the stress of the day apparent in his pale face and dull eyes. "Yes, thanks. I'm sorry to have made you jump through hoops all day for nothing. I'll have your check tomorrow."

"Don't worry about it," she said. "I'm so sorry about what happened. Please let me know if there's anything I can do for you, okay?"

"Thank you," Giles said.

Kaylee hesitated, then glanced around to make sure Nick wasn't listening. "It seems so sudden. Mitchum appeared perfectly healthy this morning. Do you have any idea how he died?"

"I only had a chance to give things a perfunctory look. I'll know more after the autopsy." Giles sucked in a breath. "I can't believe this."

"I know. It's surreal." Kaylee hesitated. "Is the convention still going to take place?"

"I think it has to. Everyone has rearranged their schedules to be here, and we have outside speakers coming in. It would seem wrong to cancel everything. Plus, Mitchum was the quintessential businessman. He'd want the show, as it were, to go on."

She nodded.

"Except for tonight," Giles continued. "I asked Thelma to call all the guests to tell them the dinner has been canceled. I hope she got in touch with everyone." He motioned to the crowd nearby. "Although there's an awful lot of people gathered here. I wonder if some of them are ours." He frowned. "Have you seen Jay?"

"No. He wasn't in or near the tent when I arrived."

"He should be here," Giles remarked. "I asked him to bring Mitchum early and take care of the dinner. I thought it would be a good opportunity for him to get more immersed in our business."

Kaylee waited, not wanting to interrupt his train of thought.

"I should have been here too, but I was busy with Mrs. Moriarty's family," he said. "It took me longer than I expected."

"Have you talked to Jay lately?"

Giles shook his head. "I assumed he had everything under control, because I didn't hear from him. I should call him and find out where he is." He pulled out his phone.

Kaylee shifted from foot to foot, not sure what to say, if anything. She hoped Jay would pick up.

Giles pressed some buttons, held the phone to his ear, and waited. Then he slipped the phone back into his pocket. "No answer."

Kaylee remembered the angry exchange that morning between Jay and Mitchum. A bad feeling slowly invaded her body, starting in her stomach and rising to her chest. She was concerned about Jay, but she didn't want to admit it to his father. "I'm sure there's nothing to worry about. He probably got called away for something. I'll check to see if his car is still there when I leave."

"Thank you. Unfortunately, I can't step away right now. We need to transport the body to the morgue."

She nodded, then led Bear to the other side of the parking lot. Jay's car was still there. She scanned the area to see if anyone was watching before she went over to it and peered through the windows.

Jay wasn't in there, thank goodness. She wasn't sure what she'd expected, but the car appeared normal. A water bottle was in the center console, and a pile of papers and a computer bag commandeered the passenger seat. A suit jacket was draped over the back of the driver's seat.

Nothing seemed to be amiss. Except that Jay seemed to have vanished into thin air.

And how exactly had he driven Mitchum here with all that stuff in the front seat?

Kaylee and Bear trekked over to her car.

After they climbed inside, she checked her phone. She had four missed calls. Two were from Reese, making sure they were still on for dinner. It was nearly seven thirty, and she'd agreed to meet him at eight. One of the other calls was from Mary, and the final one was from Jessica. She'd worry about those later. She needed Reese to know she wasn't blowing him off.

Kaylee called him back.

He answered on the first ring. "Hey. Just wanted to see if tonight still worked for you. I was about to head over to the restaurant."

"I know and I'm sorry. Today didn't go exactly as planned," Kaylee said, trying to keep her voice from shaking. She didn't want to tell him what was going on over the phone.

Clearly, Reese hadn't heard the news yet. He was way too calm. "What happened? You still want to get dinner, or should I bring something to you?"

That sounded much better. Kaylee didn't know if she could face being out in public tonight. All she wanted to do was put on comfortable clothes and sit on her couch. Having Reese's warm presence there made that sound even better. "That's a wonderful suggestion. Would you like to have dinner at my place? I'll explain it all then."

Reese sounded like he wanted to ask her more, but he didn't. "No problem. I'll be over around eight thirty with food."

"See you then." Kaylee disconnected and set the phone in her center console. Suddenly, she had a splitting headache. She realized she hadn't eaten anything since this morning when she'd had a chocolate croissant at Jessica's and then Reese's smoothie.

As Kaylee pulled out onto the street, she wondered if word had started to travel yet about the death. If it hadn't, it would soon. She mused over how long it would take Giles to figure out the cause of death. How on earth would he host a convention with all this going on? He didn't even have help right now, with Jay's whereabouts a mystery.

While she was stopped at a red light, she picked up her phone again, scrolled to Jay's number, and called him.

It went straight to voice mail.

Giles had asked Jay to drive Mitchum to the party. Had they had more words when they got there? Had the stress of a fight caused Mitchum to become ill and die? If it had, maybe Jay had panicked and taken off. But that didn't seem like him. He was in the funeral business, after all. He saw death every day. Why wouldn't he have called an ambulance? Or maybe he'd left Mitchum in the tent while he dealt with some detail for the dinner, stepped back in to discover Mitchum as Kaylee had, then panicked and left. But on foot?

Maybe she was overthinking what had happened. Perhaps someone else had been at the park, and that person had taken Jay back to the town morgue to help Giles.

She sighed. The stress of the day was getting to her. She was seeing conspiracy theories everywhere.

Kaylee pulled into her driveway, then let Bear out of the back seat and ushered him inside. She dropped her bag on a chair and went straight to the bathroom to take a shower. She hadn't actually touched the body, but she still felt dirty.

After taking a hot shower and putting on clean clothes, Kaylee felt slightly better. She worked some product through her long hair and decided to let it air-dry, then went to tidy up. She'd rushed out this morning without doing dishes. She hadn't even cleaned out the coffee maker. And Bear's breakfast bowl was still on the floor.

She got to work, loading the dishwasher, sweeping the floor, putting random things back in their places, and wiping down the counters. She finished just as the doorbell rang. She hurried to the door and opened it.

Reese smiled and held up three bags. "I brought Thai food. I always find the spiciness oddly comforting."

"It sounds wonderful. Thank you," Kaylee said as she led him into the kitchen.

Bear followed, patiently waiting for Reese to give him some attention. Reese set the bags on the counter and obliged, and Bear leaned into the affection.

Reese studied her. "Did the flower job for Giles not go well? You look like you've been through the wringer."

"The flower job went fine. It was after the flowers were done that was a problem."

He frowned. "That doesn't sound good. What happened?"

"I'll tell you when we sit down." Kaylee gathered the plates and napkins for their dinner and motioned for him to follow her into the living room.

They set the dishes and bags on the coffee table and made themselves comfortable on the couch.

Bear curled up next to Kaylee's feet. He propped his head on his paws and watched Reese open the take-out cartons and serve the food.

"Well," Kaylee said, "Mary and I spent the whole day working on the arrangements, and they turned out really nice." She smacked her forehead. "Oh no. I forgot to call Mary back. I guess I can wait until tomorrow."

"Okay, so you did the flowers," Reese prompted as he spooned curry over rice.

"Yes. Seamus delivered the centerpieces, and Mary and I made a couple extra to spread around the tent. I took the last of the flowers to the park because I had to set them up anyway.

But when I got there . . ."

Reese stared at her expectantly.

She took a deep breath. "I went into the tent and found Mitchum Landsdowne, one of Giles's fellow funeral directors, in there. He was dead."

He froze and gaped at her. "Dead?"

Kaylee nodded.

Reese set the plate down and leaned forward. "How did he die?"

"No idea. Giles needs to do an autopsy. Which must be awful for him." Kaylee got up and paced, the lovely-smelling food forgotten. "To perform an autopsy on his friend. Or colleague at the very least."

"What happened after you found him?"

"I called 911. The paramedics, Maddox, and Nick came. Then Giles, Nathan, and Abby showed up."

"What about Jay?" Reese asked.

"He was supposed to be setting up, but he wasn't there. The strange thing was that I saw his car in the parking lot."

"That is strange." Reese frowned. "What else happened?"

"Maddox worked with Giles," Kaylee replied, "and I guess they took care of everything for now. They were preparing to transport the body to the morgue when I left."

"Do you think Mitchum had a heart attack? A stroke? Did they have any preliminary thoughts?"

Kaylee's mind fluttered back to Maddox's reaction. "Not that they told me." It wasn't a lie, but she didn't know if she should elaborate on her crazy suspicions just yet. She hoped she'd be thinking more clearly in the morning after she had a good night's rest.

Reese nodded. He stayed silent for a minute, then handed her a plate. "Here. You need to eat."

Kaylee smiled. "How did you guess?" When she took a bite,

she discovered she was ravenous. "This is so good," she said between bites. "Thank you."

"I'm happy to do it," Reese said. "And I'm glad we got to do dinner despite your awful day."

"Me too." She was grateful to have such an understanding and compassionate friend in him.

Her cell phone rang. Maybe it was Jay returning her call. But when she glanced at the screen, she saw it was Mary. "I'm sorry," she told Reese, "but I have to take this. Excuse me."

"I'm sorry I didn't call you back," she said, walking into the next room. "It got a little hectic, and then Reese came over with dinner—"

"Did you know about the funeral director?" Mary interrupted.

"I did," Kaylee said softly. "I was there. I mean, I found him."

Mary gasped. "You found him?"

"Yes. When I walked into the tent to deliver the flowers, I discovered him on the ground."

"Oh, that's terrible. I'm so sorry."

"How did you hear about it?" Kaylee asked. "Is word getting around that fast?"

"Remember I'm a retired dispatcher." There was a touch of humor in Mary's tone. "Actually, the sheriff called me. He asked about Seamus and the arrangements we made."

For a second, Kaylee couldn't form any words in response. "He was asking about our flowers? Why?"

Before Mary could reply, Kaylee heard a beep signaling another call coming in. She glanced at the screen and frowned when she saw Giles's name. "Let's talk tomorrow. I have to take this call."

"See you then."

Kaylee switched calls. "Hello?"

"Have you heard from Jay?" Giles's voice held barely contained panic. "I know you were going to check to see if his car was gone when you left, but I saw it was still there. Did you happen to see him?"

"I didn't," Kaylee said. "Is something wrong?"

Reese came into the room, watching her with concern.

"I-I have to go," Giles stuttered. "Thanks. I'll be in touch." He disconnected.

Kaylee placed her phone on the counter.

"What's wrong?" Reese asked. "Did something else happen?"

"I'm not sure," Kaylee said slowly. "That was Giles. He's looking for Jay, and he sounded worried."

"Because he wasn't at the park?"

Kaylee nodded, then took a deep breath. "This morning, Jay and Mitchum argued at the bakery, and Jay stormed out. Giles told me that he asked Jay to take Mitchum to the party early. And like I told you, Jay's car was in the lot at the park, but there was no sign of him."

"I wonder what that means."

She swallowed hard, knowing that once she put it out there, there was no taking it back. "Based on what happened today, I'd bet a lot of money that Sheriff Maddox doesn't think Mitchum died of a heart attack. He was murdered. And I think the sheriff is theorizing that Jay did it."

6

After Reese left, Kaylee spent a restless night tossing and turning. She'd considered calling Mary back, but it had gotten too late. She wanted to know why Maddox had called Mary—and why he had been asking about the flowers and Seamus.

Had something come up after Kaylee left the park? Why hadn't the sheriff called her directly?

It was maddening. She tried to distract herself with relaxing music, but thoughts of Giles, Mitchum, and Jay kept colliding in her brain whenever she started to drift off to sleep. Mitchum's death had been bad enough, but Giles's phone call asking about Jay, coupled with Mary's cryptic words, had left her with an awful feeling.

So much so that when she finally gave up on sleep and crawled out of bed at six thirty, she tried Jay's cell again. She had no idea what she'd say to him if he answered and all this fuss had been for nothing. Maybe she could pretend she wanted to go running.

No, Kaylee decided. She'd be honest and tell him he'd caused a real uproar by vanishing like that. And then she'd find out where he'd disappeared to the previous night and how Mitchum had gotten to the park in the first place.

But it turned out she didn't need to worry about what to say to him, because Jay didn't answer and his phone went straight to voice mail. Again.

She left a message, then tossed the phone on the bed, letting out a growl of frustration that startled Bear. He'd still been snoozing next to her. All the excitement yesterday had evidently taken its toll on him too, and he was sleeping in this morning. At least he could sleep.

Kaylee showered and dressed, then went to the kitchen to make coffee and scrounge up something to eat. She knew she'd probably stop by Death by Chocolate, but maybe if she ate something first she'd be less tempted to order a sweet treat with a lot of calories.

It sounded like a good idea, anyway.

After eating a hard-boiled egg and drinking a cup of coffee that wasn't nearly as good as Jessica's, Kaylee dressed Bear in a polka-dot bow tie and snapped on his leash. Then the pair hustled out to the car.

It wasn't until they parked in the flower shop's lot that Kaylee realized she had a voice mail on her cell phone. It must have come in while she was in the shower. She pressed play, hoping it was Jay.

But it was Sheriff Maddox. "Good morning, Kaylee. I'll be stopping by the shop later today to ask you some more questions. Please call me back when you get a chance."

Kaylee swallowed a feeling of dread at the idea that the sheriff wanted to ask her another round of questions. She climbed out of her car and let Bear into the shop. As she headed for the bakery, she wondered what the sheriff had found out. Her gut told her it wasn't good.

She didn't have time to be dwelling on this. She had a ton of work to do today, since nothing had gotten done yesterday except the flowers for Giles's botched dinner. Maybe she should skip the stop at the café.

While Kaylee stood indecisively on the sidewalk, DeeDee pulled up and waved at her.

It was too late to leave. With a sinking feeling, Kaylee realized that everyone was going to want to talk about Mitchum.

"Good morning," she said, trying to keep her tone neutral as her friend climbed out of her car.

DeeDee rushed to her and wrapped her in a hug. "You poor thing! Are you okay? What am I saying? Of course you're not okay. You were involved in the whole awful business."

"Involved? What do you mean?" Kaylee asked as they walked to the door together. "I wasn't involved in anything. What have you heard?"

"I only meant you found the body when you were there setting up. Is that right?"

Kaylee nodded.

"That must have been horrible. I can't believe the man is dead. It seems so surreal. Just yesterday morning he was sitting here insulting Jess and ordering Jay around."

"I know."

DeeDee linked arms with Kaylee and guided her inside the bakery. "Have you heard anything else? Do they know what happened?"

"I have no idea," Kaylee said, feeling a headache starting to press against her temples. She wished DeeDee still wanted to talk about the book she'd been fixated on yesterday, but she had a new mystery to think about today—one that was not only real life but real life in their quaint town.

"Is the convention still on?" DeeDee continued.

"Yes, Giles told me he plans to keep it going." Kaylee peered around the line at the counter to see Jessica bustling around with Gretchen Cooper, her part-time employee.

Kaylee and DeeDee got in line behind two men wearing black suits. They were probably part of the funeral convention. At least Jessica was getting some business out of it.

Then Kaylee noticed someone familiar standing near the front of the line. She squinted to make sure she was seeing correctly.

Yes, she was.

Christopher Landsdowne was talking to the man beside him. As Kaylee watched, Christopher laughed.

She frowned. It seemed odd for someone who had just lost his father to be laughing like that.

"Do you have time to tell me what you saw?" DeeDee asked, jolting Kaylee back to the conversation.

"I'm sorry, but as soon as I get my coffee, I have to run. I need to get to the shop. Giles's last-minute order yesterday put us behind on everything else. Besides, I don't really know anything." She glanced around and lowered her voice. "I got to the park, and the poor man was dead in the tent."

"I'm so sorry," DeeDee said quietly.

"As for the rest of it, there's really nothing to tell. Not until the police find out something. They haven't brought me into the investigation, and I don't know whether they will." Kaylee had a feeling that she didn't want to hear whatever they found out, but it was inevitable. "It's just sad."

"Yeah, it is," DeeDee said, then lapsed into silence.

In the pause that followed, one of the two men in front of them said, "Can you believe it? I mean, of all the guys to drop dead from this job, Mitchum Landsdowne is the last one I ever expected."

Kaylee's ears perked up. They were definitely from the funeral convention. Apparently, word was traveling fast among the attendees.

"I know," his colleague replied. "What's going to happen to his empire? I heard his own son is useless." He motioned to Christopher, who now leaned against the counter placing his order.

DeeDee nudged Kaylee with an elbow. "Mitchum seemed like the type to have an empire," she whispered.

Kaylee nodded, hoping to find out why Mitchum's son was useless.

The first guy shrugged. "No clue. I heard he had a few more acquisitions in the works . . ." His voice trailed off as they stepped closer to the counter—and Christopher.

Kaylee hoped the two men would say more once Christopher got his coffee and left, but they moved to the end of the counter and continued whispering while they waited for their orders.

"How's it going?" Jessica asked when Kaylee and DeeDee stepped up to the counter. "Kaylee, are you okay?"

"I'm fine," Kaylee said. "What have you heard?"

Jessica leaned forward and beckoned them closer. "Well, Penelope was at the park when all of this went down."

Kaylee groaned. Everyone knew that Penelope Cole was a bit of a busybody. Penelope and her sister, Sylvia Rosenthal, owned The Chandlery Gift Shop located across the street from The Flower Patch, so Kaylee saw the sisters frequently. Penelope was sweet and didn't mean any harm, but she had a tendency to gossip, especially if she had information no one else did.

"She said there was a 'scandalous death' at the funeral directors' dinner," Jessica said.

"There's a chance it was scandalous, but they haven't released any official statements," Kaylee admitted. She hesitated, then went on. "Do *not* repeat this, but I think Maddox is worried about foul play."

DeeDee went pale, and Jessica put a hand to her mouth.

Kaylee nodded. "Don't say anything. I'm sure it will be public knowledge soon enough. Actually, I'm surprised it isn't already."

"Penelope also said you were at the park when all that unpleasantness happened, which was why I asked how you were," Jessica said.

"I was. But I'm late, so can we talk about it later? I have a crazy day ahead of me." Kaylee grimaced. "Although hopefully not as crazy as yesterday."

"As long as you're okay," Jessica said. "We were worried."

"I appreciate the concern, but I'm fine," Kaylee assured her. "Can I get a mocha with an extra shot, please?"

Jessica nodded. "Do you want any breakfast?"

Kaylee gazed longingly at the bakery case. "No thanks. I had an egg."

"An egg?" Jessica repeated. "After all that yesterday, I think you need something a little more substantial." She went over to make the coffee. While it brewed, she selected a cinnamon roll from the case and slipped it into a bag. "Now don't argue. Everyone knows sugar helps with shock, and goodness knows you've had one."

Kaylee laughed. So much for her intentions to be healthy this morning. She accepted her cup and pastry. "Thank you."

"We're still meeting this evening," Jessica said firmly, leaving no room for argument.

"Call me later." Kaylee said her goodbyes, then hurried to the flower shop.

As soon as she walked in, Bear darted over to her, wagging his tail.

Kaylee couldn't help but smile, though it quickly faded as she gazed around the shop and took in the wreckage from yesterday. There had been so much chaos trying to get the orders filled. And since Kaylee had left in a rush and had been detained until late the previous night, while Mary had had plans, the shop hadn't been cleaned to its usual standard.

Mary had texted that she wouldn't be in until the afternoon. Kaylee would miss her friend's brisk efficiency this morning.

Needing energy to get through the day, Kaylee took her breakfast to the counter and sat down.

Bear followed and settled by her feet. He was probably hoping she'd drop some crumbs.

The cinnamon roll was delicious, and she washed it down with a few swigs of her mocha. Nodding in satisfaction, she glanced down at Bear. "Now I think I can face the day. That egg wasn't doing it for me."

Bear yipped.

With a sigh, Kaylee thought of Maddox's message. She picked up her phone and returned his call.

The sheriff answered on the first ring. "I want to stop by today, and I was hoping to talk to Seamus McCreary when I do. Will he be there?"

"I didn't have any deliveries planned, but I can ask him to swing by the shop," Kaylee said. "Can I ask what you need with him?"

Maddox ignored the question. "That would be helpful. I'll be there around two." He hung up without waiting for an answer.

"I'd better get in touch with Seamus," Kaylee told Bear. She dragged the trash can over to the worktable in the back of the room and began tidying up while she called Seamus.

He didn't answer, so she left him a voice mail asking him to be at the shop around two. She hoped he received the message.

She'd barely made a dent in the cleanup when the bell on the shop door jingled.

Bear barked once in greeting.

Jessica poked her head in. "I had a lull, and I left Gretchen in charge. Got a minute?"

"Of course," Kaylee said. "Come in."

Jessica walked in and shut the door behind her.

Bear made a beeline to her and wagged his tail.

Jessica smiled and patted him, then turned to Kaylee. "Let me help. Hand me a broom."

"Thanks, but you don't need to," Kaylee said as she shelved the binder she'd used to point out floral arrangement suggestions to Giles. "Thanks for the cinnamon roll. It gave me new life."

Jessica grinned. "See? I knew you needed sugar."

Kaylee swept some dirt into the trash. "So what's going on?"

"I just wanted to ask you about what happened yesterday."

"You know what happened," Kaylee replied. "Mitchum Landsdowne died at the park before the party."

"Right," Jessica said. "But Joy was just in the shop and told me something interesting."

Joy Skenandore was married to one of the sheriff's deputies, and Kaylee wondered what kind of inside information she had relayed to Jessica. "What?"

"She said the police are searching for Jay Akin."

7

Kaylee froze. Was that why Giles had called her in such a panic last night? "Why are the police searching for Jay? Did Joy tell you?"

"I'll bet it has something to do with Sheriff Maddox suspecting Mitchum Landsdowne didn't die of natural causes," Jessica answered. "She said Jay's car was at the 'scene of the crime,' but he was missing. She sounded worried. Like she wanted to try to find him herself and tell him he was in trouble, bless her heart."

That sounded like Joy. She took on the problems of everyone in town as if they were her own. She was one of the people who made Kaylee feel like the town was one big family. And everyone loved the Akins.

Jessica's eyes were wide with concern. "Do you think it's true? Was Mitchum really murdered?"

"I don't know. I found him dead on the ground. We'll have to wait for the autopsy."

"I guess you're right." Jessica walked around the shop, stopping to peruse the lavender goat milk soaps DeeDee made. Aside from the obvious flowers, the beauty products were at the top of many customers' lists. Jessica picked up a bar and sniffed. "This smells amazing. It has a stronger lavender scent than the last batch."

Kaylee nodded. "DeeDee said she used more in this one and added a touch of essential oil. She called it an experiment."

DeeDee also made creams, candles, and lovely sachets. Kaylee was thrilled to sell her friend's handcrafted products at The Flower Patch.

"It's lovely. I'm buying it," Jessica announced as she brought it up to the counter.

"Take it," Kaylee said. "On the house. My register isn't open yet anyway."

"No." Jessica pulled out her wallet and opened it.

"I'm giving you the friend's discount," Kaylee said. "Don't argue. You didn't let me pay for that roll this morning. And I know DeeDee would agree."

"Thank you." Jessica dropped the bar and her wallet into her purse. "So what do you think about Jay?"

"What do you mean?"

"If it's true that Mitchum was murdered, do you think Jay could have had something to do with it?" Jessica raised an eyebrow. "You saw them yesterday. Jay wasn't exactly getting along with the man."

"Come on. We know Jay. How could you even ask that?" Kaylee said, trying to ignore the concern worming its way into her brain. Jay had seemed very angry and uncomfortable with Mitchum yesterday. What was really going on there?

"I know you two are running buddies," Jessica said, "but how well do you actually know Jay?"

"Enough to know he's not a killer." Kaylee sighed. "Look. No one knows for sure what happened to Mitchum yet. Let's not convict Jay before we do, okay? Plus, there were other people around the party site."

"Who?"

"The bartender, who seemed like an angry guy in general. And my delivery guy. Sheriff Maddox wants to talk to him."

Jessica hesitated, then said, "Someone in the bakery last week said that Jay got arrested."

"Jay? I don't believe it," Kaylee scoffed. "I can't imagine him doing anything illegal. What happened?"

"Disorderly conduct," Jessica stated. "Something about a fight at a bar. He was unruly and ended up getting arrested."

Kaylee was taken aback. "That doesn't sound like Jay."

Jessica shrugged. "I don't know what to tell you. That's what I heard."

That was troubling. What on earth was going on with Jay?

"Have you talked to him since yesterday morning?" Jessica asked.

"No. I tried to call him, but I haven't been able to reach him," Kaylee replied. "I hope he's okay." Then another thought, an even more frightening one, entered her mind. "What if Mitchum was murdered, and something bad happened to Jay too?"

Jessica stared at her, her face draining of color. "You mean, you think someone . . ." She obviously couldn't bring herself to say the words.

"I don't know. I don't even want to think about it." Kaylee rubbed her hands over her face. Good thing she hadn't bothered with makeup today.

"That's terrifying," Jessica remarked. "We can't have a serial killer running loose on the island."

"There's no serial killer running loose. Don't freak out on me."

"You said it," Jessica reminded her.

"I know, but I didn't sleep well last night."

The shop bell jangled, and Bear barked.

A stocky young man with straw-like hair and a short beard stepped inside, glancing around with pale-blue eyes in a broad face. "So this is your shop, Kaylee."

Kaylee gasped. "Jocko?"

Bear ran up to the newcomer, tail wagging.

Jocko McGee knelt and rubbed his ears. "Hey, buddy. Nice to see you too."

"What are you doing here?" Kaylee asked. She'd met the reporter when she'd helped with the flowers on the set of a movie that was being filmed on Orcas Island. He'd been hoping for a scoop.

Jocko came over and shook her hand, then Jessica's. "I'm freelancing for *The Orcas Gazette*. It's not a big gig, but it helps to pay the bills, you know?"

Kaylee had a feeling the hungry reporter wasn't here on a social call. She might as well get to the point. "What can I help you with?"

Jocko grinned. "I heard there was an unattended death at the park last night and that my old pal was there. Not only there, but you found the body. I'm here to get some information. You know, present your side of the story and all. It'd be great publicity for the shop."

Kaylee couldn't see how being involved with a murder—again—would do anything for her business. "I'm sorry, but I have no comment. The police would be your best bet," she said, even though she knew that Sheriff Maddox would toss the reporter out on his ear.

Jocko's grin remained in place, but there was a shrewd gleam in his eye that she didn't like. "Aw, come on. I understand that you don't want to comment on the way the guy died since the police are still investigating. But while I wait for more information from them, I was hoping to get a few comments on the scene itself. I'm gathering some color for the story. You know how it is. Readers want to feel like they were actually there."

"I'm sorry," Kaylee repeated, "but I have no information for you. It would be completely inappropriate for me to comment about anything to do with last night."

Jocko didn't seem discouraged by Kaylee's refusal. "I'll be back when the police have released their statements so you don't feel like you're leaking anything. In the meantime, I can always go see what I can find out from the funeral directors about their esteemed colleague. Coworkers are always good for gossip about someone's life."

"I'm not sure you can count on gossip with this group," Kaylee cautioned. "They're used to keeping things confidential for clients."

"Sure, but he wasn't their client, and I'm so charming. Besides, they're used to dealing with reporters to publish obituaries. I'm sure someone will have plenty to tell me." Jocko strolled back out of the shop, whistling.

Jessica faced Kaylee. "He's not wasting any time."

"No," Kaylee said, reaching down to pet Bear. "I guess he figures this is going to turn into a front-page story once the police determine the cause of death." She had a sinking feeling it wasn't going to be natural causes.

After Jessica left, Kaylee juggled cleaning the workroom and waiting on her customers, while privately counting down to Mary's arrival. People seemed to be out and about in full force, and Kaylee didn't know if it was because the weather was nice or because they wanted to talk about Mitchum Landsdowne's murder.

The weather idea turned out to be just wishful thinking on her part. All morning Kaylee tried to dodge questions from customers who wanted to discuss the unfortunate incident.

Kaylee loved Turtle Cove and the interactions she had at the shop, but sometimes small-town life was exhausting. With Mary out, her day was hectic enough without having to listen to the continuous rehashing of a man's death.

By lunchtime, after she fended off a persistent customer's questions and gave her a free bottle of body lotion to get her out the door, she had a good mind to lock up and go home early.

"I wish you could be my guard dog," she told Bear, "but you're way too sociable."

Bear wagged his tail and gave her his huge doggy grin, proving her point.

"Should we run over to The Sunfish Café and grab a sandwich?" Kaylee asked him.

Bear's ears perked up at the mention of food.

"That seems like a yes to me." Kaylee smiled and picked up his leash.

A ride and some fresh air did her good. Kaylee and Bear took the long way to the café, where she ordered a catfish sandwich with some chips and an iced tea to go.

She parked overlooking the water and found she'd regained a little of her appetite, so she ate half her sandwich and shared some fish with Bear. She wished they could sit here for the rest of the day and ignore everything else.

Kaylee glanced at the clock in the dashboard and sighed. "We'd better get back to work. Mary should be in, and we have the sheriff to deal with."

Bear lay down in the back seat and covered his face with his paw.

"My sentiments exactly," she said.

When she pulled into the parking lot at the shop, a police cruiser was in her usual spot.

Sheriff Maddox waited at the door, holding one of her flower arrangements from Giles's canceled dinner party.

Maddox was early. Maybe he wanted to speak to her before he talked to Seamus.

Kaylee swallowed. She took her time parking and collecting her bag, then let Bear out.

He scampered over to the sheriff, tail wagging.

Maddox bent down and scratched his head.

"How are you today?" Kaylee asked when she joined them.

"Fine." But Maddox didn't look fine. He appeared exhausted, as if he'd been up all night. Maybe he had.

"I wasn't expecting you until two," she remarked.

"I wanted a little time with you before I speak to your deliveryman. How are you doing?"

"Good. Bear and I were just getting back from lunch."

The sheriff glanced around the empty parking lot. "I was surprised to find you closed. Are you alone today?"

Kaylee nodded. "We closed for an hour so I could get something to eat. It was only Bear and me this morning, but Mary should be in shortly. I think she wanted to avoid cleaning up yesterday's mess." She smiled to show she was kidding.

Maddox didn't smile.

Kaylee didn't say anything else as she picked up Bear's leash and led him and Maddox inside the shop.

The sheriff set the flowers, which had begun to droop, down on the counter. He also held a little plastic bag. "I need to ask you about the floral arrangements you did for Giles's dinner event."

"What do you need to know?" She tried to keep her tone matter-of-fact, but she could hear the nerves creeping in.

"Can you tell me what the flowers are?"

"Sure." Kaylee leaned over the flowers, touching the petals. "*Dahlia hortensis*. Or just dahlias." The dahlia was one of her favorite flowers. Dahlias traditionally represented elegance and dignity—two traits a funeral director should represent, which was why she had suggested them for the convention dinner.

Mary had chosen purples, whites, and yellows for the color scheme. They were bright and beautiful—perfect for an elegant summer dinner party.

"This arrangement was to be a centerpiece, as you probably

already know," Kaylee continued. "Dahlia is the main flower, and we also put some lavender and traditional greenery in them."

"Anything else?" Maddox persisted.

"Let me check Mary's notes to see if she added anything different to any of them. We didn't want to create identical arrangements. We felt it would have been too dull for the mood Giles wanted for the event." Kaylee went to the worktable, hoping to find Mary's notes buried in the remainder of the mess somewhere. Mary was great at documenting what she used for each project.

The sheriff studied the arrangement while he waited.

Kaylee searched under pieces of ribbon, stems, and other debris and finally pulled out a couple of notebook pages, stained green from flower cuttings that had ended up on top of them. "Here we go." She returned to the counter and jabbed a finger at the blue flowers in the center of the sketch. "These are *Aquilegia caerulea*. Blue columbines. They set off the purple nicely."

Maddox remained silent.

Kaylee spoke up again. "Why are you asking?"

Instead of answering, Maddox held the papers up and perused them, then regarded the arrangement again. "Are you sure there's nothing else in here?"

"Like what?" Kaylee asked.

The sheriff sighed and leaned against the counter.

Before he could speak, the bell over the door jingled.

Bear barked, and then Marianne Crosby, a longtime customer, walked inside.

Kaylee hurried over to her. "Good afternoon," she said brightly.

"Good afternoon, dear." Marianne glanced curiously at Maddox. "Hello, Sheriff. Are you fighting crime at the flower shop?" She giggled at her own joke.

"How can I help you?" Kaylee asked.

"I need a bouquet to take to my friend Rosemary at the nursing home," Marianne replied. "She's feeling down today, and I need something to cheer her up."

"How about these?" Kaylee steered her to the cooler and pointed to a joyful bundle of daisies. "I can do these up with a nice balloon. Or maybe a stuffed animal."

Marianne brightened. "A stuffed cat would be nice. She had to let her cat go live with her daughter. They won't let her have Mr. Fuzzball at the home. It's criminal, I think. Don't you think so, Sheriff?"

"I'm sorry," Maddox answered, "but I really can't comment on the nursing home's policies."

"That is terrible," Kaylee said. "Everyone should be able to have their pets." She held up a stuffed orange cat. "How about this guy?"

Marianne pursed her lips. "Do you have a gray one? Mr. Fuzzball is gray."

After Kaylee selected the right color cat and made up a bouquet, she sent Marianne on her way and shut the register. Then she turned back to the sheriff. "So where were we?"

"Seamus McCreary. Is he coming in?"

"I left him a message."

"Did you tell him I wanted to talk to him?"

"No, I just said I needed him here around two."

Maddox nodded. "What do you know about Seamus?"

"Not much," she admitted. "He's here visiting family and wanted to make some extra money. He stopped in and asked if I had any work."

"Did you check him out at all before hiring him?" the sheriff asked. "Do you know where he lives? Who his family is?"

Kaylee felt her face redden. She hadn't. It was probably shoddy business practice on her part, but she hadn't thought about someone who wanted to deliver flowers as a potential danger to society. When she'd lived in Seattle, she doubtless would have run an extensive background check on him, but she'd let her guard down since moving to Turtle Cove, where people treated each other like family and were exactly as they seemed. Maybe she believed too much in the goodness of people. "I didn't. And no, I don't know where he lives or who his family is."

Maddox gave her a stern look.

"What?" she asked defensively. "I pay him cash when he does a delivery. It's not like he's making big money here. I didn't know you worked for the IRS."

"Not funny. This is a serious matter."

"I'm sorry," Kaylee said. "I give him mainly jobs that involve company deliveries, not personal ones. I handle most of those myself or ask Mary to do it." She started feeling nervous because of the sheriff's persistent questions. "Why are you asking?"

Maddox reached for the little plastic bag he'd been carrying. "Do you know what this is?" he asked, holding it out.

Kaylee took the bag and studied the plant through the plastic, noting the stem with a leaf and some dark berries on it. She recognized it immediately as the *Atropa belladonna* plant, which in her opinion had a unique beauty to its flowers when blooming in the wild.

"That's called deadly nightshade and for good reason. It's one of the most toxic plants in the world," she replied, setting the bag down on the counter. "It's certainly not something any florist worth his or her salt would keep hanging around the cooler to add to arrangements. Where did you get it?"

"The coroner I called in from Seattle finished the autopsy on Mitchum last night," Maddox said. "We've sent out some toxicology tests, but I'm pretty sure we're going to get our theory confirmed. I wanted to check with you."

"What theory is that?" Kaylee asked.

"I believe our guest didn't die of a heart attack. He was poisoned with nightshade."

8

"Poisoned," Kaylee repeated, dread flooding her body. The theory of murder had been floating around, but hearing it directly from Sheriff Maddox was startling. "How? And why did you bring in another coroner?"

"First of all, Giles was exhausted," Maddox said. "And I was concerned that his worry over his missing son would affect his work. I gave him a break on this one. The coroner believes Mitchum drank something he shouldn't have."

The bowl of red liquid sitting innocuously on the table last night at the party site popped into her mind. "Are you talking about what was in the punch bowl? Was the whole thing poisoned?" That could mean something entirely different than if just Mitchum's cup had been tampered with.

"Whoever killed him only laced his cup, which we can't find anywhere," the sheriff answered. "The punch in the bowl was fine, but the coroner found traces of plant matter in the punch in Mitchum's stomach."

Kaylee motioned to the little plastic bag on the counter. "What about the nightshade?"

"I found it on the ground. I'm guessing it fell out of a larger bunch."

"I see," Kaylee said, struggling to keep up with the news.

"How quickly could it poison someone who drank a concoction made out of its berries or whatever parts are poisonous?" Maddox asked.

"It depends on how much was used," Kaylee said. "A higher dosage would probably bring on symptoms pretty quickly."

"How easily available is nightshade?" the sheriff asked.

"It grows in the woods around here. If you know what to look for, you can definitely find some. And I'm sure it's not terribly hard to research." She paused. "Although I can think of so many easier ways to kill someone."

Maddox raised his eyebrows at her cryptic comment.

"Do you really think Seamus went out into the woods to pick deadly nightshade, then added some to the punch in the park and gave it to Mitchum? I can't fathom it." Kaylee shook her head, flummoxed, picturing the mild-mannered Irishman who'd shown up at the shop one day, asking politely if she had summer work.

The sheriff didn't respond.

"Why would Seamus do that?" Kaylee went on. "How would he even know Mitchum?"

"That's what I need to figure out," Maddox said. "Finding out more about who Seamus is would be the biggest help right now. When did he contact you for a job?"

Kaylee thought back. "It was about two or three weeks ago."

"Interesting timing," he said.

"Not if he's planning to be here for the summer. People will start showing up for vacations soon," Kaylee reasoned. "Nothing about Seamus suggested to me that he was dangerous."

"He might not be dangerous to the general public, but he might have a reason to be dangerous to Mitchum," Maddox said. "He hasn't called you back today?"

"No, but it's not strange. I usually just leave him messages. He doesn't seem very chatty in general."

"If he's in town only temporarily, he could take off anytime," the sheriff said. "For all we know, he could have already left on this morning's ferry."

The door opened, making the bell jingle.

Bear barked and raced to the door to greet Mary as she walked in.

She smiled and bent down to scratch behind the dog's ears. When she turned to Kaylee and Maddox, her smile faded. "My goodness. What's going on?"

"We're waiting for Seamus," Kaylee said quietly.

"I see. He's coming?"

"I left him a message."

"I was telling Kaylee that Mitchum Landsdowne was murdered," the sheriff said.

Mary sucked in a breath. "I was hoping that theory was wrong."

Kaylee had a thought. "What about the bartender?" she asked. "Kurt seemed really cranky in general. And since it was a beverage that was used to poison Mitchum—"

"I questioned the man for a while after you left last night," Maddox said. "I don't think he had anything to do with it. Plus, there was no alcohol in that punch, so he had no reason to be near it."

"Does he have an alibi?" Kaylee asked.

"I'm going to confirm with his place of employment what time he left for the job," the sheriff replied. "But I'm guessing based on what I can piece together that he got there later than my killer would have."

The three of them lapsed into an uncomfortable silence.

Then the bell jangled, and once again, Bear barked.

Seamus McCreary rushed in, taking off his hat, leaving his red hair sticking up. "Sorry I'm late, Miss Bleu," he said breathlessly. "I just got your message. I was away from my phone. Hi, Mrs. Bishop."

"Hi, Seamus." Mary smiled, obviously trying to put him at ease.

"Thanks for coming," Kaylee said. "Do you know Sheriff Maddox?"

Seamus shook his head and took a step back. "Should I?"

"No, I was just wondering," Kaylee said. "I'm not sure if you heard, but there was an unfortunate incident last night at the park where we were setting up for that dinner."

"I didn't hear anything," Seamus responded. "The funeral people?"

Kaylee nodded. "Sheriff Maddox wanted to talk to all of us because we were involved with the flowers, and you and I were on-site at different times yesterday."

Seamus's already pale face lost even more color.

Maddox stepped forward. "I'd like to hear about when you got to the park yesterday, if you saw anyone, what you did. Standard questions when we have a crime." His tone was matter-of-fact, but his eyes were hard.

Seamus swallowed. "A crime?"

"Yes, a visitor to our town was poisoned," the sheriff stated.

Seamus's mouth worked, but nothing came out. He glanced from Maddox to Kaylee to Mary, then back to Maddox. "I-I don't know any of those people," he stammered.

Maddox turned to Kaylee. "Is there somewhere Mr. McCreary and I can talk privately?"

Kaylee pointed to the stairs. "You can use my office."

"Thanks." Maddox motioned for Seamus to go first.

The other man climbed the stairs slowly, as if he'd suddenly lost all his energy.

The sheriff followed Seamus upstairs.

"That poor man," Mary murmured. "I hope this is nothing."

"Me too. I can't believe it." Kaylee picked up Bear and hugged him tight. "I feel like there could have been so many people around there yesterday that no one would even know about. It was in the middle of the park, for goodness' sake."

"I know. It's troubling." Mary glanced at her watch and sighed. "We should try to get some work done."

"You're right. Let's tackle the order for that retirement party. It should come together pretty quickly," Kaylee suggested.

Kaylee set Bear down, and she and Mary got to work on the order in silence.

It seemed like ages before Seamus and Maddox walked downstairs. Neither looked happy.

"I take it you don't have a job for me?" Seamus said to Kaylee.

"Not today. But I'll be in touch later in the week, okay?" She offered him an encouraging smile.

Seamus seemed dazed as he put his hat on and left.

Kaylee and Mary turned to the sheriff.

"He's free to go, then?" Kaylee said. "That's a good sign."

"For now," Maddox said.

"Oh no. You really don't think he had something to do with it, do you?" Mary asked.

Maddox didn't reply.

"Did you find out who his family is?" Kaylee pressed.

"Clay Tucker is his distant cousin."

"Clay? The fisherman?" Kaylee was surprised. Clay was a bit rough around the edges, probably from spending so much of his life out on the ocean. It was a tough profession. She was having a hard time picturing Seamus related to him.

"Yes. They're related on Clay's mother's side of the family. They met during a family reunion a few years back. Seamus said he'd always wanted to visit Turtle Cove, so he's staying here with Clay." Something in the sheriff's tone suggested that he didn't quite buy the whole story. Or maybe there was a part of it he wasn't telling them.

"If that's true, then maybe he was simply in the wrong place at the wrong time," Mary suggested.

"Maybe so," Maddox said, but he didn't sound entirely convinced. "We'll see. Thanks for your time, ladies."

Kaylee reached out to stop him from leaving. "Sheriff, wait. Do you really suspect Seamus? Should I not hire him for deliveries anymore?"

Maddox studied her for a long moment. "Just be careful," he finally said. "For all intents and purposes, there's a killer loose on the island."

As soon as Maddox left, Kaylee said quietly, "Well, that didn't sound good."

"It certainly didn't. Oh, I forgot to tell you," Mary said. "DeeDee asked if we could move our meeting to tomorrow. In all the chaos, she forgot that she's hosting an event for Giles and his crew at the bookshop tonight. Some kind of reading. One of the funeral directors published a book of essays on grief and loss."

"Interesting," Kaylee said. "Perhaps we should go."

Mary tilted her head, and the corners of her mouth curved up. "You mean to get the lay of the land?"

"To support DeeDee and Giles." Kaylee paused. "And maybe a little to assess the landscape."

Mary smiled. "I'm in."

"Great. Speaking of Giles, I'm going to run over and see him. Do you mind?"

Mary shook her head. "Not at all. I'll be here."

"Thanks," Kaylee said, then turned to Bear. "Do you want to go for a ride?"

The dog didn't hesitate. He ran straight to the door.

Kaylee grabbed her purse, snapped on Bear's leash, and headed out to her car.

First, she needed to make a call. She stopped on the porch and took her phone out of her bag. When she tried Jay's number, it went to voice mail again.

Kaylee stood for a minute, tapping her phone against her thigh, wondering exactly what was going on. Where was Jay? Had he vanished on purpose? Or was he not able to answer?

If he wasn't able to answer, she didn't want to think about

what might be preventing him.

She shivered. Had he bumped into Seamus at the park? Did he know something?

Kaylee loaded Bear into the car, then pulled out onto the street, glancing at Death by Chocolate. She noted the nearly empty parking lot. It was the afternoon lull.

If there was a new development in the case, she fully expected Jessica to call or show up at her door again to fill her in. Jessica had the advantage of hearing a lot of the island gossip and happenings early on. Sugar and caffeine encouraged a good deal of conversation.

But Kaylee didn't want to be peppered with questions or theories right now, so she didn't stop. She needed to talk to Giles.

When she arrived at the funeral home, she noticed the hearse parked outside. A pile of purple funeral flags lay on the hood. She thought of Mrs. Moriarty. It would be too soon for her funeral if she'd just passed away the day before. She wondered if Giles had another customer in the house.

Then she remembered Mitchum. His body was probably here in the morgue. The thought gave her the chills. She wondered when Mitchum's son would take him home. Christopher certainly hadn't seemed to be too grief-stricken when she'd seen him that morning.

She immediately felt guilty for the thought. People grieved differently, and she shouldn't judge a man she didn't even know.

As she pulled up to the curb, Giles emerged through the side door, staring at her curiously as she got out of the car and opened the door for Bear.

If Sheriff Maddox had appeared tired, it was nothing compared to Giles. Normally, the funeral director wore neatly pressed clothes, but today his black pants and dress shirt were rumpled, almost as if he'd slept in them.

If he'd actually gotten any sleep.

Bear tried to rush over to Giles, but his leash held him back.

"Easy, Bear Dog," she murmured, then waved at Giles.

"What brings you here?" Giles seemed to be making a desperate attempt to sound normal, but Kaylee could tell the man was physically and emotionally drained.

"Sorry to come by unannounced," Kaylee replied. "Do you have a minute to talk?"

Giles glanced behind him at the building, then nodded. "Why don't you come inside?"

Kaylee and Bear followed him in through the side door. They walked through the casket and urn showroom and into the main hallway, then into the small seating area on the first floor—a room set aside for anyone who wanted a temporary escape from the wake or funeral service.

The design of the funeral home was well thought out, and the atmosphere welcomed people like a hug when it was most needed. It was no wonder Giles's place had such a tremendous reputation in the area.

Kaylee sincerely hoped this debacle wasn't going to hurt him professionally, given the questions swirling around Jay.

"Please have a seat," Giles said. "Can I get you some water?"

"No thanks." Kaylee perched on the edge of one of the chairs.

Bear curled into a ball at her feet.

Giles sat down across from her, but he looked like he was ready to spring up at any second and run.

She figured it would be better to cut right to the chase. "Sheriff Maddox visited me at the shop today."

Giles raised his eyebrows but said nothing.

"Have you talked to him?" Kaylee asked.

Giles hesitated. "He let me read the preliminary autopsy report."

"He told me Mitchum was poisoned."

Giles sighed. "That's what appears to have happened. Did Maddox come see you because of the type of poison?"

Kaylee nodded. "He also questioned my delivery guy about whether he tampered with the drink when he delivered the centerpieces."

"Who is your delivery person?"

"Seamus McCreary. He's in town for the summer. Maddox found out he's distantly related to Clay Tucker and is staying at Clay's."

Giles frowned but didn't reply.

She couldn't keep the questions in any longer. "What's going on with Jay? Have you heard from him?"

"No, and I'm terribly worried," Giles admitted.

"Me too." Kaylee leaned forward. "I just tried calling him again and got no answer."

"I haven't been able to get ahold of him either," Giles said. "I have no idea where he could possibly be."

Kaylee laid a hand on his arm. "I'm so sorry. I can't imagine what you and Thelma are going through."

Giles gave her a small smile. "Usually I'm the one saying something like that. It's strange to be on the other side of it." He stared back down at his hands. "I just wish we had a way to clear Jay's name."

"I think the only way to do that would be to find out who actually killed Mitchum. Do you know if he had any enemies?" Kaylee asked, knowing the sheriff had probably already asked him that exact thing.

When Giles didn't answer right away, she tried to convey the urgency she felt. "He seemed like a strong personality when I saw him with Jay."

Giles flinched.

His reaction told her there was more to be said about that, but he clearly didn't want to tell her. Which only made her want to know even more. But she must exercise restraint. He was more likely to simply shut down and ask her to leave if she bombarded him with too many questions at once.

"Giles," she said quietly, "I want to help. Please talk to me. How well did you know Mitchum? Was he a friend? I can't imagine how hard it must be to do an autopsy on someone you knew."

"I've had to do it before. Death is simply the next chapter, you know." Giles stood and turned his back to her, staring out one of the windows. "I've known Mitchum for a long time," he finally said. "Professionally, of course. We weren't friends or anything."

"What did other people think of him?"

"He was very well respected in the community, and he often served as a mentor to the younger folks entering the profession. I admire his business sense greatly. He was incredibly successful, and he's been a valuable resource for many people in the industry."

It sounded stilted to her. But Kaylee waited, sensing that he was about to say more.

"Who am I kidding?" Giles spun and met her gaze. "Mitchum was not a nice man. He was loathed. And I think there were plenty of people who wanted him dead."

9

Although Kaylee didn't like to admit it, she wasn't exactly surprised to hear that Mitchum had been so reviled. "The fact that plenty of people wanted Mitchum dead could be good news, right? It will help the sheriff's department realize Jay is innocent."

"Theoretically," Giles said. "But as long as my son is still missing, it looks bad for him. I have no way of proving that people wanted Mitchum dead. When I say that, it sounds like I'm only trying to deflect suspicion from Jay."

"What was Jay's relationship with Mitchum?" she asked. "Was he working on something for the conference with him?"

"Yes. I feel terrible that I gave him the task, but I needed the help. Also, it comes with the territory." Giles spread his hands. "This is the job. It's really just the two of us and Thelma, and there are many things involved with it. Sometimes there are more things to be done than hands to do them."

"Jay seemed miserable, and Mitchum's son wasn't even paying attention," Kaylee said. "By the way, how did Christopher react when he heard the news about his father's death?"

Giles pursed his lips. "He didn't have much of a reaction, I'm afraid."

"Really? What is he doing now?"

"He's staying over at the inn. He told me he'll remain in town until he can take the body home. He also said his father would want him to focus on the business and the convention as much as he could." Giles's tone suggested he thought that was absurd, but he didn't comment on it.

"I wondered," Kaylee said. "I saw him at the bakery this

morning, having coffee and laughing with one of the other men from the convention. What's the deal with him?"

Giles wrinkled his nose, and Kaylee guessed that he, like the two men she'd seen that morning, had very little use for Mitchum's son. "He's part of his father's business. But Mitchum made all the money already, so he doesn't have to work very hard."

"What does he do?"

"Christopher runs one of the funeral homes in Seattle," Giles replied. "He's more like a figurehead. The actual work there is done by others under him. From what Mitchum told me, the business basically runs itself, so it's a foolproof job."

"It doesn't seem like Mitchum put much faith in his son," Kaylee remarked.

"Christopher blew some significant deals a long time ago," Giles explained. "That was when Mitchum learned he couldn't give him any important jobs in the business."

"Mitchum confided in you about his son?"

"No. We talked business," Giles said. "Christopher is part of the business, and most of the time I think Mitchum thought of his son only in business terms."

"It sounds like they weren't close," Kaylee said.

Giles shook his head.

Kaylee hesitated. "Was Mitchum married?"

"No, he got divorced a few years ago. Since then, he'd had a different date every week."

Before she lost her nerve, Kaylee blurted, "Could Christopher have had anything to do with his father's death?"

"Why, I have no idea," Giles said, sounding taken aback.

"Well, he was in town, right? He probably was with his father for most of the day." Kaylee stood and paced. "Where were all the convention attendees yesterday? Were they all in one place?"

"Unfortunately, no. Some of them got in Sunday night, and

others trickled into town yesterday. My doors were open for people to congregate here, but I really don't know who was here and who wasn't."

"When did Mitchum arrive?"

"Sunday night. He liked to arrive early so he could check things out," Giles replied.

"Do you think he had any idea someone might have a problem with him?"

"No, and I suspect that was due to his ego. I don't believe Mitchum bothered considering how his actions affected anyone else. It would never occur to him that anyone would want to do him harm."

"What exactly were his actions?" Kaylee asked. "Why did everyone hate him?"

"Mitchum was ambitious and greedy, and he had a big ego. He wanted to be the king of the funeral business, and he bought out as many smaller homes as possible."

"Did he acquire those businesses for the money?"

"I'm not sure," Giles said. "I think he might have done it more to be noticed and admired."

"Was he admired?"

"To an extent, I suppose," Giles responded. "But he was blind to the fact that people who knew him well or who'd been on the receiving end of one of his takeover attempts weren't so happy with him."

Kaylee considered the long list of suspects. Then another thought struck her. "Did he try to buy you out?"

"Of course not."

Kaylee believed he'd answered too fast, but she didn't press the issue. She wasn't sure she wanted to know. The answer might have implications for Jay.

"I'm sorry the sheriff dragged you into this. I'm sorry *I*

dragged you into this," Giles said, rising from his chair. "But we'll have to wait and see how it plays out."

"You didn't drag me into it," Kaylee said. "It just happened, and now we have to find Jay. I can't believe he did anything wrong, and the quicker we find him, the quicker it gets sorted out. I want to help. Plus, if my delivery person had something to do with it, I need to know."

The relief was apparent in his eyes. "Thank you."

Kaylee picked up Bear. "Please let me know if I can help in any way. Especially since you're still working on the convention in the midst of it. Just remember you've got a support system that will jump in wherever needed."

"I know. We have a wonderful community here." A hint of a tired smile appeared on his face.

"When are you starting the convention?"

"Our workshops begin at one o'clock today, and we're hosting a dinner tonight," Giles answered. "Everything else will go mostly as planned, but we're extending the event to make up for the late start. Everyone has the option of staying through Sunday for meetings and networking instead of wrapping up on Friday morning."

"I hope it goes smoothly. I'll let you know if I hear from Jay. I've left him a few messages."

"If I hear anything, I'll be sure to tell you," Giles said. "I know you two are friends. He talks about how nice it is to have someone to run with. He says you motivate him."

Kaylee smiled. "He's the motivator. I would have given it up ages ago if not for him."

She bid Giles goodbye. As she and Bear hurried outside, her mind worked overtime. She wondered exactly what Christopher's deal was, and more importantly, what his relationship with his father had been like. Had it been as bad as Giles thought?

Or had it been even worse?

Thanks to DeeDee's interest in mysteries, she'd heard her fair share of stories—both fictional and real—where parents were too hard on their kids or the kids were unstable, with dire consequences.

Had Mitchum's ambition and his son's lack of it been a major point of contention? Enough to drive the younger man to murder?

Christopher hadn't seemed all that engaged in whatever had been going on with Jay and Mitchum in the coffee shop yesterday. She'd hoped Giles could tell her what that had been about, which was why she'd nudged the conversation in that direction, but no luck.

And Jay wasn't around to tell her.

Which left Christopher.

Kaylee loaded Bear in the car and climbed in, then paused to think. She knew it was horrible for Maddox to even have to consider Jay a suspect, given the relationships here on the island, especially with Giles.

Even though the sheriff was curious about Seamus McCreary, Kaylee knew he'd consider himself remiss if he didn't pursue all the angles.

She wondered if that included Christopher.

Then she sighed. Now she was jumping to conclusions. Kaylee didn't want to imagine she could have hired a person who would poison someone, and she couldn't believe her friend could intentionally hurt anyone, no matter what the gossip mill claimed. Was she just entertaining the idea of Christopher's possible guilt because she didn't want to face the idea that one of the two young men she liked might have killed someone? She didn't know Christopher at all. How could she assume he was capable of murdering his own father?

This whole thing was so frustrating. The not knowing, the

worrying about Jay, the uncertainty about Seamus. She felt like she needed to *do* something.

She picked up the phone and called Mary.

"Are you still at the shop?" she asked when Mary answered.

"Yes. Is everything okay?"

"Would you like to take a ride with me?"

"Sounds mysterious," Mary said. "Do I want to know?"

"I'll pick you up in ten minutes. I'll explain then." After Kaylee disconnected, she glanced behind her into the back seat.

Bear wagged his tail. He seemed to be enjoying this week's adventures.

She was glad someone was.

And they did have another adventure ahead. Hopefully one that would help her figure out who killed Mitchum.

Mary waited outside the shop when Kaylee drove into the parking lot eight minutes later.

"You're early," Mary teased as she climbed into the car.

"You're waiting, which must mean you're excited." Kaylee winked and pulled back out onto the street.

"Where are we going?"

"Northern Lights Inn."

Mary raised her eyebrows. "Why are we going there?"

"To see Christopher Landsdowne."

"And we need to do that because . . . ?"

"Because Giles said Christopher and his father didn't have a good relationship." Kaylee glanced at Mary. "I wonder if he had anything to do with his father's death."

"You're going to ask him? Sheriff Maddox will have your head."

Kaylee shrugged. "At least Christopher might give us some answers."

Mary was silent for a moment. Then she said, "Jess and DeeDee are going to be upset we didn't bring them along on this excursion."

Kaylee smiled. That was Mary's way of saying she was on board. "Jess is working, and DeeDee has her event tonight. That reminds me. Are we still going?"

Mary nodded. "Can't we wait and see Christopher there?"

"What if he doesn't show up?"

"So what's our excuse for stopping by the inn?"

"I needed to see Reese," Kaylee answered, "and I heard he was doing a job there."

"It's as good an excuse as any," Mary said. "Are you going to simply ask to see Christopher?"

"I'll figure it out when we get there," she said. "Have you learned anything else today?"

Mary sighed. "It's been hectic. Although I'd rather not hear all the gossip, people have been calling me all day to tell me more. I finally had to set my phone to do not disturb."

"Really?" Kaylee tried not to appear too curious. "Who's been calling you? What have you heard?"

Kaylee suspected Mary could get more information than pretty much anyone else in town. As a former dispatcher for the police department, as well as having a friendly relationship with many of her previous colleagues, Mary was in a great position. Since she was discreet and trustworthy, it made it even easier for people to confide in her or answer questions. Kaylee had seen both of these traits at work many times since she and Mary had become friends.

"We're almost to the inn. I'll tell you on the way back." Mary turned to her and grinned. "I don't want to distract you from your strategizing."

When they pulled into the inn's parking lot a few minutes later, Kaylee didn't think it would be that hard to find anyone. It looked like the entire funeral contingency was having their networking hour outside. It was hard to blame them given the beautiful weather.

"This might be easier than we expected," Kaylee said. She checked the back seat. Bear was asleep, so she figured she'd leave him that way. She cracked the windows and got out of the car.

Mary glanced around the parking lot. "I don't see Reese's truck."

"That's okay. He's only our excuse for being here," Kaylee reminded her.

"Good point," Mary said.

They walked through the parking lot. Kaylee scanned the men gathered in small groups, searching for Christopher.

"Bummer," she whispered to Mary as they reached the door. "I don't see him."

Mary held the door open for her, and they stepped into the lobby.

The inn had a nautical theme with lots of blue and white with hints of gold. Kaylee spotted tasteful anchor and ship's wheel motifs dotted around the room, but she still saw no sign of Christopher.

She tugged Mary into the small restaurant area off the lobby, crossing her fingers. But it was empty except for two guys sitting at the bar.

"Go try asking at the desk," she urged Mary.

"What? Why me?" Mary asked.

"Because you have that trustworthy mom face."

"Gee, thanks," Mary said drily. But she pasted on a smile and approached the desk.

Kaylee watched as Mary talked to the clerk.

The clerk seemed to respond. She picked up the phone,

listened, then shook her head.

Mary frowned as she walked back to Kaylee. "Christopher is staying here, but he's not in his room, or at least he's not answering his phone," she reported.

Kaylee let out the breath she'd been holding. "We might as well go."

"Well, it was a good idea," Mary said as they headed back to the car.

When they climbed inside, Bear poked his head between the seats.

"Did you have a nice nap?" Kaylee asked, straightening his bow tie.

The dog wagged his tail.

As Kaylee prepared to back out of her space, she glanced in the rearview mirror. She spotted a red Prius entering the parking lot. It seemed familiar.

Then her mouth dropped open. It was the same one Seamus McCreary used for deliveries. As she watched, Nathan Anghelone stepped out of the passenger seat and slipped into the crowd.

"What's wrong?" Mary asked.

"Did you see that?" Kaylee watched the Prius as it slowly drove out of the parking lot. She put the car in gear. She had to know if it was Seamus.

Mary stared at her. "See what?"

"Nathan just got out of Seamus's Prius." She followed the car down the street.

"Seamus told Maddox that he didn't know any of the funeral directors," Mary said. "So what on earth is he doing with Nathan?"

10

Kaylee tried to keep at least three car lengths behind the Prius. She wasn't sure if Seamus would notice her tailing him, but she figured it was better to be safe than sorry.

"Why are we following Seamus?" Mary asked.

"I want to make sure it's him," Kaylee said, "and I'm curious about where he's going. Do you think he's really staying at Clay's?"

Mary shrugged. "It's easy enough to find out, so I'm not sure why he would make it up. Especially to the sheriff."

Kaylee wasn't sure about anything anymore. She kept her eyes glued to the Prius. If it was Seamus and he was going to Clay's, then the turnoff was nearby.

Sure enough, a minute later the Prius's blinker went on and the car turned right, heading down the narrow road to Clay Tucker's beachfront cabin.

Kaylee pulled off to the side where she had a clear view down the short road.

The Prius stopped in Clay's driveway, and Seamus climbed out. There was no mistaking his red hair.

Heart pounding in her throat, Kaylee got back on the road. "It was definitely him."

Mary nodded. "What do you suppose that's all about?"

"I have no idea. Do you think Nathan broke down on the side of the road and Seamus happened by to pick him up?"

"Too convenient," Mary said.

"Yeah." Kaylee sighed. "I thought so too." Then she remembered Mary had some things to tell her. "You were going to fill me in on what else you heard today."

"Ah yes. I spoke with Thelma Akin," Mary said. "She's very worried about Jay."

"So is Giles."

"That's right. You stopped to see him earlier. How is he?"

Kaylee shrugged. "As well as can be expected."

"You haven't heard from Jay yet, have you?" Mary asked.

"No. I've left him some messages, but he hasn't returned my calls."

"Thelma is trying not to be an alarmist," Mary continued, "but she feels she has reason to be concerned about Jay lately. He's apparently feeling pressured about his role in the business, and he's been rebelling a little, for lack of a better word. After all, he is an adult, so I don't know if you can really call it rebelling."

Kaylee couldn't hide her surprise. "Really? I thought he was happy to take over his dad's business." Jay had never sounded like he resented his career path. But like most people, he probably had a public face and a private one.

"That was my impression too. Thelma and Giles have been adamant about Jay's propensity for the business. But Thelma told me that he's been withdrawing from them and putting in only the minimum amount of effort. I do wonder if he's been a victim of his family's good intentions." Mary paused. "He's also had some trouble with the police."

Kaylee stilled, rolling to a stop at a red light. "Jess told me that, but I hoped she was mistaken."

"Unfortunately, she wasn't. A friend on the force told me that Jay was arrested for disorderly conduct a few weeks ago."

"Jess said that Jay got into a fight at a bar."

"Yes, Jay and some other guy were throwing punches at each other." Mary shook her head. "It's too bad."

"Who was Jay fighting with?" Kaylee asked.

"I don't know the other man. Someone from out of town, I think. I heard they were fighting over a woman."

"Jay doesn't seem like the type to get into a fistfight over a woman," Kaylee said doubtfully.

"I thought the same," Mary said, "but there's no denying it happened."

No denying it happened was one thing, but the real reason could have gotten lost in translation. "Who was the woman?"

"My friend didn't say," Mary said.

Kaylee pulled up in front of The Flower Patch. "Okay, so maybe Jay did get into a fight. So what? A scuffle over a woman doesn't mean that someone suddenly morphs into a murderer. But it seems like that's the road the police are going down. I understand that it's troubling given the way Jay vanished, but still."

"Of course it doesn't mean he's a murderer," Mary said. "But if he's having some kind of personal problems lately and they're making his behavior escalate into something abnormal, then it's cause for concern. Looking at it objectively, I can see that argument."

"Sure, I guess," Kaylee agreed reluctantly. "But why would he all of a sudden not want to be involved in his dad's business?"

"Good question," Mary said. "Maybe he's simply getting to the age where he realizes his own choices, his own desires, have been pushed aside in favor of wanting to please his family. And maybe he's fighting that, at least on a subconscious level. I'm sure the sheriff has to consider it very carefully."

Kaylee couldn't help but think of Jay's car, parked alone in the lot at the park last night. With Jay nowhere in sight and Mitchum dead on the ground. And no word from Jay since. Was his silence because he had a reason to hide?

"I know Jay and Mitchum had words yesterday morning,"

Kaylee said. "But why is everyone so ready to jump to the conclusion that Jay could kill someone?"

"I don't know," Mary admitted. "I assumed that whole business at the bakery was related to the convention. I heard the planning for it has been all-consuming. I thought Jay seemed miserable. He must have been tired of having too many masters. But to be mad enough to kill?"

"I don't believe it for a second," Kaylee said. "Do you?"

"No," Mary said.

"We have to find out how Seamus knows Nathan and what they were doing together. And if Christopher Landsdowne could have been involved. I mean, for all we know, any of the funeral directors could have done it."

"What do you mean?"

"Giles told me that Mitchum had tried to take over other funeral parlors," Kaylee replied. "He had a lot of business dealings with people, and there could have been some bad blood."

Mary opened her door. "The event tonight at the bookstore should be interesting."

"I'll pick you up shortly before seven."

As Kaylee drove home, she concluded that something was off in Turtle Cove.

She was relieved to be heading for the sanctuary of Wildflower Cottage, even if it was for only a couple of hours. Kaylee really wanted to put on her pajamas and curl up with a mindless romance movie or read a book and eat junk food until she felt better. But she had to get ready to go to the reading. Plus, her mind wouldn't stop spinning with everything that had happened.

She also realized she'd missed a call from Reese while she'd been out. But when she called him back, it went to voice mail.

As soon as Kaylee and Bear walked through the door, the dog trotted over to his bowl and glanced up at her.

"Are you trying to tell me something?" She grinned as she poured kibble into his bowl.

Maybe she'd be able to think more clearly if she had something to eat too. She slid the leftover Thai food—which also made her think of Reese—into the microwave and sat down on the couch with her computer.

While she waited for her food to heat up, she called the sheriff's department.

Aida Friedman, the receptionist, answered the phone.

"It's Kaylee," she said. "Is the sheriff around?"

"So nice to hear from you." Aida dropped her voice. "Crazy things going on around here, right?"

"Definitely," Kaylee agreed.

"I think the sheriff is just getting off the phone," Aida said. "Hold for a moment, please."

Kaylee waited impatiently for Maddox to pick up.

When he did, he sounded guarded. "What can I do for you?"

"Seamus McCreary knows Nathan Anghelone," she blurted out.

There was silence on the other end of the phone.

"Hello?" she asked.

"I'm here. How do you know this?"

"I saw Seamus dropping Nathan off at Northern Lights."

"What were you doing at the inn?" Maddox asked.

She remembered the excuse she'd come up with for just this question. "I was trying to find Reese. He has a job there." *Well, at least he did,* she amended in her head. Besides, he might still be there. For all she knew, Reese had fixed the leak and stayed on at the inn to work on other odd jobs around the place.

"What a coincidence," the sheriff remarked.

Kaylee decided to change the subject. "Didn't Seamus tell us that he didn't know any of the people here for the funeral convention?"

"He told me that," Maddox said. "I don't know about 'us.'"

Kaylee sighed. The sheriff got prickly like this sometimes, usually when he felt someone was butting in on one of his cases when he hadn't asked them to. "So are you going to find out about it?" she pressed.

"I will definitely look into it." His stiff tone told her that he was annoyed she knew something he didn't.

"Oh, did you learn anything about the bartender?" Kaylee asked.

"Not that it's your business, but I confirmed he hadn't yet left his place of business when the poisoning would have had to have occurred," Maddox said. "One suspect down. Now I have to get back to work." He disconnected.

Her microwave beeped. She removed her food and carried it into the living room, along with a pad of paper and a pen. Making lists had always helped her data-driven mind solve problems more easily. Otherwise, all her thoughts kept swirling into each other, and she had a tough time separating them into coherent pieces that made sense.

She sat down on the couch with Bear tucked up next to her and jotted down what she knew so far.

1. Mitchum was killed.

2. Maddox thinks Mitchum was poisoned by Atropa belladonna.

3. Jay was supposed to be at the park setting up when the alleged poisoning happened. His car was there, but he was nowhere to be found—under suspicion.

4. Jay and Mitchum had words at the café Monday morning while Mitchum's son, Christopher, seemed to ignore them.

5. Christopher and Mitchum reportedly didn't have a close relationship.

6. Seamus had access to the dinner site while no one else was around.

7. Giles asked Jay to take Mitchum to the park, but it didn't look like Jay did because there was no room in his car.

8. Seamus knew Nathan well enough to drive him around, even though Seamus says he's new to town and told the sheriff he didn't know any of the people attending the convention.

9. Giles says Mitchum had a lot of enemies.

10. Jay has been having some trouble lately, including with the police, and he seemed to be losing interest in his family's business.

Kaylee set her pen down and perused her list. It was random, and it made her head hurt. Nothing seemed to be in any kind of order that she could see. Had she forgotten anything? There were a lot of gaps in her list, but if she could have filled them in, she would have solved this by now.

A few names jumped out at her: Seamus, Nathan, and Christopher. Though she hated to acknowledge it, so did Jay's. The bartender was off the hook. Which left three viable suspects, because she couldn't believe for one second that Jay had done anything wrong.

So it all came back to Seamus, Nathan, and Christopher. The three names swirled in her head as she polished off her food.

Then she grabbed her laptop and did a search for Mitchum

Landsdowne. There were a ton of hits on the guy. Mitchum was certainly the don of the funeral business in the greater Seattle area. Fascinated, she scrolled through the mentions and began learning about the murder victim.

Mitchum had started out with one funeral home that his father had run very modestly. He'd taken over the business at age twenty-four after his dad became ill and couldn't continue working full-time.

Within two years, Mitchum had expanded to another two funeral homes. He bought out the local places that hadn't been doing well and turned them into thriving businesses. By the time Mitchum was thirty, he owned five funeral homes and was a partner in three others. And he hadn't stopped there.

Kaylee scrolled through newspaper articles where Mitchum had been interviewed. She read news releases on the deals and customer reviews of some of the establishments. Everyone who went to one of Mitchum's funeral homes seemed more than satisfied with the service. A few people even gushed about Mitchum and how successful he was, and one person went so far as to refer to him as a legend in the funeral business.

Mitchum had also started a mentoring organization for young professionals. According to an excerpt Kaylee read, the funeral business was hard to break into unless the person had family ties, and Mitchum had always thought that was unfair. He said he wanted to give young people who had an interest in the profession every opportunity to succeed even if they didn't have a legacy to help them through the door.

And he'd given many people that opportunity. He'd even backed a couple of younger people who'd had the opportunity to buy a business but couldn't get the financing they needed. Given what she'd learned from Giles, Kaylee assumed that Mitchum had been glad to have the additional income streams while they paid him back.

From all she'd read, Mitchum was nothing if not a shrewd businessman. So was his charity really a part of who he was, or was it all an act, a way to advertise his own services? Someone had wanted him dead and wanted it badly enough to see it to fruition. Was it someone to whom he'd refused financing? Someone who had to rely on him for funding and didn't want to? Someone who was behind in payments?

Had Mitchum turned this merger and acquisition endeavor into a kind of mafia deal? Was the funeral business really that cutthroat?

Kaylee continued scrolling, searching the images related to Mitchum as well. There were a few with Christopher, mostly in a funeral setting. One image showed the two of them posing next to what appeared to be a new limo. Another showed Christopher looking on while his father shook hands with another man and a crowd of people clapped. It must have been some good deed or important deal he'd closed, Kaylee surmised.

It was fascinating to see Mitchum evolve from an eager young man to the magnate with the expensive shoes and commanding air she'd met at the bakery. That image was quickly replaced by the image of him dead on the ground in the tent, and she shivered.

When she did a search for the funeral directors' convention, a whole new slew of photos and articles popped up. Mitchum had apparently hosted the event three years prior, and it had been a big deal in the funeral world. Magazines and newsletters dedicated to the trade had covered the event, and Mitchum had been the featured funeral director in an industry magazine.

Kaylee wondered if the rest of the conventions were as heavily attended and covered as that particular event seemed to be. This year's convention was definitely not in the same league. There had been an influx of people to Turtle Cove but not nearly the numbers of three years prior. She chalked up the buzz around

Mitchum's convention to Mitchum himself.

She clicked through the pictures slowly, not sure exactly what she was searching for, but it seemed important to get a sense of Mitchum's life.

She paused at a group photo from that popular convention and zoomed in. Some of the faces seemed familiar.

Yes, there was Nathan, standing off to the side. He was watching Mitchum, and she couldn't see his face well enough to read his expression. He seemed to have a good deal more hair and fewer lines in his face then, even though it was only three years ago. Maybe this business aged people quickly.

Or maybe something else had taken its toll on Nathan. Had he done business with Mitchum? Had their dealings gone south? Maybe Mitchum had set his sights on Nathan's business, and Nathan didn't have the finances to fend him off.

Or maybe he and Mitchum had been working together, and something went awry.

Kaylee leaned forward and drummed her fingers on the coffee table. Nathan had seemed calm and laid-back, but she reminded herself that business and money could drive people to do terrible things.

Had Mitchum and Nathan been doing a business deal together? Had something gone wrong—wrong enough for Nathan to want Mitchum dead?

The more she thought about it, the more her heart raced. Nathan had been involved in the party planning. He'd been right there with Giles for the details. He'd known when the tent would be set up and when people, including Jay, would start arriving.

In short, Nathan had opportunity.

But did he have the motive too?

And how could she find out?

11

Kaylee assumed Sheriff Maddox had Nathan on his radar. He had to. Nathan had been around all day yesterday, and Maddox was especially interested in people who had been in or near the tent shortly before Mitchum's death. She wondered if Maddox knew that Nathan had worked with Giles on the convention. Surely that would pique his interest.

Then she was reminded of seeing Nathan and Seamus together at the inn. Were they in cahoots somehow? How did Seamus fit into this? Was he really here to visit Clay, or was Maddox right and the timing of his appearance was a little too convenient?

All these thoughts were making Kaylee uneasy. It was hard to believe there was someone in their midst who was capable of taking another person's life. It was especially disturbing to think that she might have hired a killer to work for her at the flower shop.

Kaylee scribbled a couple of notes on her list, adding these questions, then turned her attention back to the computer.

Her cell phone rang, startling her. She glanced at it and saw that it was DeeDee.

"What's up? Are you okay? I haven't had a chance to talk to you. I'm dying to hear everything. What's going on with our dead guy?" DeeDee didn't even pause for breath.

Kaylee could barely keep up. It made her smile, even in the midst of all the crises. "Don't you have an event to set up for?" she asked.

"I'm multitasking," DeeDee said. "Are you coming?"

"Yes, and so is Mary." Kaylee winced. "Oh no, I forgot to call Jess."

"Don't worry about it," DeeDee said. "I already told her she needed to come, and she's on her way."

Kaylee glanced at the clock and gasped when she saw the time. "I'd better get a move on. I'll fill you in later."

"I'm holding you to it," DeeDee said. "See you soon."

Kaylee hung up, and within ten minutes she had washed her dishes and changed into a decent pair of jeans, a long-sleeved T-shirt, and a pair of boots. Then she gave Bear a few treats and a kiss and promised him she'd be home soon.

She picked up Mary, and they headed for Between the Lines, which was just down and across the street from The Flower Patch. It was nice to have everything so close together.

They arrived as the funeral contingency began to pull up. Kaylee didn't see Giles, but Nathan was there, helping direct people to the folding chairs that DeeDee had set up in the open space at one end of the shop. He waved when he saw her.

Trying to ignore her suddenly elevated heartbeat, she left Mary chatting with DeeDee and Jessica and walked over to Nathan to say hello.

"How's the convention going?" she asked. "Is everyone doing okay?"

"We're trying to keep everything as normal as possible. No one went home, which is a good sign." He kept glancing at the door and straightening his flashy purple tie as he talked. "Are you here for the reading?"

"Yes, and to give DeeDee moral support." Kaylee caught DeeDee's eye.

DeeDee raised her eyebrows in a question.

Nathan grinned. "I told her she needs to start carrying more books written by funeral people. There are some good ones out there, and it kind of fits with her subject matter, don't you think?"

"It does. Especially since a lot of mysteries center around deaths." Kaylee grimaced as she realized what she'd just said. "Sorry. Like we all need a reminder of that right now." But maybe this was the door opener into the conversation she wanted to have about Mitchum.

Nathan sobered. "We deal with death every day, but I think it gives us a different perspective when it's one of ours, you know?"

Kaylee nodded. She opened her mouth to speak, thinking she'd start by asking him about Seamus, but he glanced beyond her and beamed, and she turned to see Abby entering the shop.

"Excuse me," Nathan said, then moved around her to join his wife.

Kaylee wanted to protest, but she figured she could catch Nathan after the reading. If she made a big deal out of it now, it might seem suspicious when she wanted to appear casual. She wandered over to her friends.

"What's going on, Nancy Drew?" Jessica asked, giving her a nudge. "You have that look in your eyes."

"Let's go somewhere we can talk in private," Kaylee said.

"I knew there had to be more to your sudden interest in essays by a funeral director," Jessica remarked.

"Come on," DeeDee said. "Most people are still arriving, so we have a few minutes to talk."

Kaylee, Mary, and Jessica followed her to the back room.

DeeDee shut the door behind them, blocking out the chatter from the store. "So what's going on? Is this about our dead guy?"

"Yes, it's about the dead guy. I don't know that he's *our* dead guy." The thought made Kaylee's stomach roll.

"Well, what about him?" DeeDee asked. "Was he really poisoned? Are there any leads on who did it?"

Kaylee blew out a breath. "We have plenty of leads.

Unfortunately, they start with Jay, because no one's heard from him since yesterday."

DeeDee's mouth dropped open. "What? Are you serious? I heard the rumors about Jay, but I didn't think they meant anything."

"They don't mean anything," Mary stated. "As soon as Jay turns up, he'll clear it all up and explain that he had nothing to do with it."

"I agree," Kaylee said.

Jessica didn't seem so sure.

"What?" Kaylee asked her.

"I don't know," Jessica said. "We all love Giles, but I'm not sure if anyone really knows Jay that well."

"I do. Kaylee does," Mary protested.

"Kaylee runs with him," Jessica said, "but that means they're probably too busy trying to catch their breath to talk much."

"Good point, but I'd still like to think I would know if he had the ability to kill someone. But regardless, there's something weird going on with Nathan." Kaylee lowered her voice and told them how she and Mary had seen Seamus drop Nathan off at the inn.

"That definitely sounds suspicious," DeeDee said.

"Then there's the whole matter of Mitchum's son, Christopher," Kaylee continued. "Giles thinks he didn't get along with his father."

"After seeing the way Christopher ignored his dad in the bakery, I'm not surprised," Jessica said.

"Giles said a lot of people loathed Mitchum," Kaylee went on. "His words, not mine."

"Any other leads?" DeeDee asked.

"Maddox came to the shop to question Seamus today," Kaylee replied. "It really shook him up. I couldn't tell if it was because he was shocked to be questioned or if he has something to hide."

"So we have three suspects," Jessica concluded. "Nathan, Christopher, and Seamus."

They were all quiet for a moment.

DeeDee checked her watch. "I'd better get back out there. We'll continue this later, okay?"

"We'd better," Jessica said.

They joined the group out in the bookstore. DeeDee went to the front of the room, and the others took seats in the back.

Kaylee studied the attendees. It was a good crowd. She estimated about twenty-five people had come to listen to the reading.

She didn't see Giles, but she wasn't expecting him to show up. If Jay was still missing—and she hadn't heard otherwise—then Giles must be beside himself. She knew he would put aside his host duties in a heartbeat to try to find his son.

Sitting back, Kaylee let her mind wander over the puzzle pieces. None of them seemed to fit, and she felt like she was missing something important.

Then her thoughts were interrupted when a man in a black suit got up and read depressing essays in a dry monotone. She couldn't help but wonder how someone in the funeral business could spend his days not only dealing with the dead but then going home and writing about it.

She tuned it out as best she could, letting her mind continue to mull over the puzzle.

It seemed like only a few minutes later when the reading ended and people began to get out of their seats. She must have been tuning out even more than she'd thought.

Small pockets of serious-looking men stood around talking while DeeDee collected the folding chairs.

Kaylee went over to the other side of the room to help her friend.

Nathan and Abby joined her.

"Where do these go?" Nathan asked, holding a few chairs

under each arm.

"In that back room." Kaylee pointed to a door behind them. "Where's Giles tonight?" she asked.

Nathan sighed and set the chairs on the floor. "He wanted to be here, but he has so many other things on his mind, as you know. Especially with Jay—" He stopped and dropped his gaze.

"With Jay missing," Kaylee said. "I know it's scary."

"Well, it's not only that Jay's missing," Nathan said. "It's also that he's been somewhat . . . unpredictable lately."

Kaylee frowned. "What do you mean?"

"It's like he's had a sudden change of heart about working at the funeral home, and he doesn't want to help out with the convention. Then he was publicly disrespectful to Mitchum, an important colleague." Nathan shook his head. "Jay's been kind of falling apart. He's having a temper with his family and flying off the handle over little things. His dad is worried. And so am I."

"I keep hearing variations of this story," Kaylee said, "but it doesn't sound like Jay."

"I know what you mean," Abby said. "It's not like him at all."

"That's why Giles thought Jay might have some kind of medical issue," Nathan explained. "He begged his son to get checked out, but Jay brushed it off."

Kaylee gasped. "You mean mental illness?"

Nathan nodded.

Kaylee couldn't believe what she was hearing. Granted, she didn't know Jay as well as the people who spent nearly every day with him, but he had never seemed unstable to her. In fact, he seemed quite the opposite. And she knew how much he loved his family.

Plus, this conversation was sidetracking her from her chance to ask Nathan questions about Mitchum and Seamus.

"This all sounds out of the blue to me," she said doubtfully.

"It did to me too until Jay started talking to me," Nathan replied. "It wasn't just Giles. I was hearing firsthand from Jay how much he was struggling with things."

"Jay was confiding in you?" Kaylee asked.

"Yes. I've been a close friend of the family for a long time."

"I think Jay sees Nathan as an uncle," Abby said.

Nathan nodded. "Sometimes I believe it's easier for him to talk to me than his dad."

"So what kinds of things was Jay telling you?" Kaylee asked. "Was it that he didn't want to work at the funeral home anymore?"

"It was several things," Nathan admitted. "Work, personal. He was having a hard time. Please don't repeat any of this. I'm telling you because I know you're friends with him. If you have any idea where he might be—"

"Of course I would tell Giles," Kaylee interrupted. "But I haven't heard a peep from Jay either."

"I hope he comes home soon," Abby said.

"It's making it so much worse for his parents," Nathan said. "And if the sheriff decides that he has enough evidence against him for Mitchum's murder, this could get ugly."

"Well, I hope he doesn't," Kaylee said. "But I do have a question for you."

Nathan looked at her inquisitively. "Shoot."

"Seamus McCreary," she said. "You know him?"

Nathan didn't respond at first. Just as she was beginning to wonder whether he would, he said slowly, "I met him a couple of weeks ago."

"Where?" Kaylee asked.

"He did a delivery at Giles's funeral home one Sunday while I was there," Nathan said. "Nice guy."

Kaylee was about to ask him more, but DeeDee walked over. "I'm sorry I forgot to call you back," she told Abby. "Our next class is Monday."

"Wonderful. I can't wait." Abby smiled. "It'll be a great weekend activity to do with our kids."

DeeDee nodded. "My girls love helping me with it."

"I didn't know you were teaching," Kaylee said to DeeDee. "What kind of class is it?"

"I'm sorry. I kept meaning to tell you, but we've had so much else to talk about that it kept slipping my mind. I've been calling it DIY with DeeDee," she said, her eyes lighting up. "We've done workshops on making your own soaps, lotions, and other beauty products with natural ingredients and things you can find around your house. We recently did one about how to add wildflowers to your own soaps, and we discussed which ones are beneficial, which ones are just beautiful, and which ones are dangerous and should be avoided. There are three more workshops in the series."

"The class is small, only about six people," Abby said, "and I've been learning so much in the last few weeks. DeeDee is an amazing teacher."

"I'm glad you're enjoying it," DeeDee said.

"It sounds interesting," Kaylee remarked.

"Your grandma would remember that we used to do things like this in the Petal Pushers years ago," DeeDee told Kaylee. "It's part of our original mission to bring our love of flowers into the community."

"That's great," Kaylee said, recalling Abby's excitement the day she'd visited the shop with Nathan and Giles.

"I love it," Abby said. "Thanks for doing it, DeeDee."

Nathan put the folding chairs away, then came back. "We have to head out, but thanks again for hosting the reading tonight."

Abby smiled at Kaylee and DeeDee. "See you later."

Nathan offered Abby his arm, and they walked out together.

"What was that all about?" DeeDee asked. "Nathan seemed serious."

"I was asking him if he knew Seamus," Kaylee said.

"And?"

"He said he met him when Seamus did a delivery at the funeral home a couple weeks ago on Sunday," Kaylee said.

"Well, that makes sense," DeeDee said.

"Not exactly."

"Why not?"

"We don't make deliveries on Sundays."

Herb picked up Mary and took her home, so Kaylee went out to her car alone. She climbed in and locked the doors. The whole business had left her unsettled in her own skin. Why had Nathan lied about when and where he'd met Seamus?

She drove the short distance slowly, her mind still working through the facts. She pulled into her driveway and gazed at Wildflower Cottage, silhouetted against the night sky. At least she'd had the foresight to leave some lights on so the place wasn't totally dark.

On impulse, she grabbed her phone and made a call.

"Sheriff's department. Deputy Garcia speaking."

"Hi, Robyn. It's Kaylee Bleu. Is the sheriff around?"

"Hey, Kaylee." Robyn Garcia's voice warmed. "How are you holding up?"

"I'm okay," Kaylee answered.

"Good. The sheriff isn't here. May I take a message?"

"Please have him call me," Kaylee said. "It's about Mitchum Landsdowne."

"Anything I can pass on?"

"I heard something tonight that I wanted to tell him about," Kaylee said. "I also had a question. Maybe you can answer it."

"I'll try," Garcia said.

"Did anyone figure out how Mitchum got to the park? The only vehicles there were the caterers' van and Jay's car."

"I believe the assumption is he came with Jay," the deputy said, lowering her voice. "But I'm not sure." She hesitated. "They impounded Jay's car and are searching it for evidence, so I guess we'll know soon."

"I saw inside Jay's car. There was stuff piled in the front seat. Papers and such. It seems like it would have been hard to have a passenger."

Garcia made a noncommittal sound. "I'm not really in on the investigation, and Maddox would have my hide if I shared anything without his permission anyway. You know that. I'll have him call you, though, and you can see what you can get out of him. Hang in there, okay?"

Kaylee thanked her, then hung up and got out of her car.

A feeling of unease swept over her as she hurried up the walkway. *I'm being silly,* she chided herself. Her imagination was running wild. Given the events of this week, it was understandable, but she hated it when she let her mind get the best of her.

Then she realized Bear was barking.

Racing to the door, she inserted her key in the lock with shaking hands. It took her two tries to unlock it. She burst through the door. "Bear?" she called, trying not to sound as frantic as she felt.

Her little dog dashed into the room from somewhere in the back of the house. He stopped several feet away, still barking, and refused to come closer when she called him.

Panicked now, Kaylee locked the door behind her and kept her phone in her hand as she crept through the house.

Bear followed close at her heels, still barking.

"What's going on, Bear Dog?" She tried to keep her voice calm, but she knew she wasn't doing a good job. She debated calling Reese, but she figured that would make her seem insane at worst and hysterical at best.

After all, there couldn't be someone in the house. Could there? Bear would be acting even stranger. Although the way he was acting now reminded her of his behavior at the park when he'd tried to alert her to Mitchum's body.

But if there was someone here, where would the person be hiding?

Swallowing against the panic in her throat, Kaylee continued through the house. She loved the cottage and its location. It was slightly off the beaten path and surrounded by wildflower fields with the majestic Turtleback Mountain in the distance. But right now she felt alone and exposed.

Bear ran to the windows in the living room and barked more frantically.

Kaylee followed and stared at what appeared to be a light in the distance. Was it from her neighbor's house? No, she couldn't see the house on that side of her that well. And even if she could, the light was coming from the wrong place.

She shivered. Was someone out there watching her?

12

Heart pounding in her throat, Kaylee raised her phone again, ready to give in and call Reese.

Then the light outside disappeared.

She squinted but couldn't see it any longer. "Bear, what was that?" she asked softly. "Was someone outside? Is that why you were barking?"

Bear gazed up at her, tail wagging. He seemed calmer now, as if any danger, either imminent or imagined, was over. It made her feel only slightly better.

She went back through the house, double-checking that all the windows and doors were locked. For the time being, she decided against calling Reese.

But there was no way she was going to bed yet. Or maybe ever. Instead, she lit a fire in the fireplace and grabbed a blanket.

Bear jumped up next to her on the couch and snuggled close, as if sensing that she needed his presence.

She tried to read, but she kept getting distracted by every little sound. Finally, she gave up and switched on the TV, finding a fluffy romance movie to keep her company.

It was after two o'clock when she fell into a restless, light sleep on the couch, her phone still clutched tightly in her hand.

Early the next morning, after a night of uneasy tossing and turning, Kaylee woke up to the sun streaming through the cracks in the blinds and a massive crick in her neck from her position on the sofa.

She got up, trying to work the soreness out, and opened the blinds so she could peer outside. In the daylight, her terror from the previous night seemed silly. There was nothing out there but her lovely lavender and a beautiful, sunny day.

But the sense of unease lingered.

She checked her phone. Still no word from Jay or anyone else for that matter.

She stepped outside into the loveliness of the morning and picked up the week's edition of *The Orcas Gazette*. Any good feelings she'd been cultivating disappeared when she saw the article on the front page with Jocko McGee's byline under the title.

Coroner's Son Chief Suspect in Rival's Murder

Kaylee scanned the article, dread dropping into the pit of her stomach as she went back inside.

> *Jay Akin on the run after apparently demonstrating an unconventional way to drum up business for this week's convention for funeral directors . . . hasn't been seen since the morning of the incident . . . Friends and family refused to comment, which can only mean that they suspect him just like the sheriff's office . . .*

Kaylee slammed the paper down on the table, stormed into the kitchen, and dumped some food into Bear's bowl. Then she made her own breakfast, paying little attention to what it was or how she was preparing it. *That Jocko!* How could he justify publicly condemning someone he didn't even know?

After she showered and dressed, she put a sky-blue bow tie

on Bear, then got him in the car and headed off to the shop. She might as well put her furious energy to good use.

She needed more coffee, and she needed to check in with her friends and see who was taking Jocko's implications seriously. She dropped Bear off at the shop, then walked to the bakery.

DeeDee and Jessica were camped out at a table in the corner. They appeared to be in deep discussion.

Kaylee walked up and sat down. "What did I miss?"

"Lots of talk about Jay, even without that article this morning," DeeDee said in a low voice.

"Really? Why?" Kaylee held her breath, hoping there had been no new developments that actually incriminated him.

"I'm not sure," DeeDee answered. "It's just flying around how he was at the park and how he's been difficult lately. I don't know where these rumors are coming from."

Kaylee thought she might have a good idea. She shook her head, thinking of Nathan's words last night. The more time that went by, the more worried she became about Jay. "I wish I knew if he was okay. He needs to get back here so he can clear his name."

"I know. It's very sad," Jessica said. "I wonder where he could be."

"The only places I usually see him are the park for our runs and here at the bakery," Kaylee said. "But I'm sure those are the last two places he'll show up." She sighed. "I feel awful for him."

"What's really going on with Jay?" DeeDee asked.

"I heard he was questioning his life path," Kaylee said. "But that's natural for a twenty-five-year-old. I think he's trying to find his way. We all go through it. If he was acting out because he doesn't know how to be heard, it's a call for help."

"I agree, but his family is so lovely," Jessica said. "Why wouldn't he be able to talk to them?"

"You know how that can be," Kaylee said. "Sometimes

families have high expectations. It makes things hard."

They were quiet for a moment.

Kaylee broke the silence. "Are we having our meeting tonight?"

Jessica leaned forward, a twinkle in her eye. "We thought we'd go to dinner and crash the funeral guys' party instead."

Kaylee brightened. "Really?"

"Yes. They're meeting at The Ideal Meal. And wouldn't you know it—suddenly I have a hankering for that place myself."

Kaylee grinned. "I'm in. But I need a coffee so I can go plow through my day."

"Come on," Jessica said, motioning toward the counter. "I'll let you cut in line."

"Thanks. Can you do a latte, maybe with extra espresso?" she asked her. "I need a jolt."

Jessica nodded. "Coming right up. So what do you think about tonight?" she asked as she got the coffee ready.

"I think it's brilliant," Kaylee said. "How did you find out?"

"I hear things," Jessica said with a wink, capping Kaylee's latte and handing it across the counter.

"Should we make a reservation?"

Jessica laughed. "I might have already done that. We'll meet there at seven thirty."

When Kaylee got to the shop, she was relieved to see Mary's car already in the lot. She hoped the store was quiet today. She wanted to talk some of this through with her friend.

As soon as she pushed the door open, Bear ran over to greet her.

Kaylee grinned and scratched behind his ears. She stashed her purse behind the counter, then headed to the workroom.

Mary was arranging pink and white roses in a slim pink vase at the worktable. She looked up from her task and smiled. "Good morning. How are you doing today?"

Kaylee shrugged. "I'm okay. Didn't sleep well," she said,

thinking of the light flashing in the woods behind her house. But she didn't want Mary to worry, so she didn't mention it. "You?"

"I'm okay too," Mary said. "It was such an interesting evening last night."

"I'll say." She leaned against the table and sipped her coffee. "What do you make of this thing with Nathan and Seamus?"

"Well," Mary said, "I did find something out."

Kaylee's ears perked up. "Really?" She glanced behind her at the shop door, hoping no one showed up to interrupt this conversation. She'd kept the door locked, but they would have to open soon. And she really wanted to hear what Mary had to say. "What did you find out?"

"The sheriff got more intel on Mitchum's business practices."

Kaylee felt her heart rate pick up. "Is this based on the information Giles had about him?"

Mary nodded. "Giles has been filling the sheriff in, and Maddox has been talking to many other people, including the funeral directors staying on the island this week. He's really glad the convention wasn't canceled."

"I'll bet," Kaylee said. "Easier access. Is he talking to Mitchum's son too?"

"Yes. I know Maddox has been stalling on releasing the body because he doesn't want Christopher to leave yet."

"That's good." Kaylee knew Sheriff Maddox was great at his job, but she was relieved to hear it from Mary. She was also grateful for her friend's contacts—and the trust she inspired in people to get this kind of information.

"You read that Mitchum was quite the businessman," Mary continued, selecting some yellow roses from a pile on the table. "He loved to talk about his business dealings. Acquiring funeral homes and building an empire meant everything to him."

"In my research, I discovered that Mitchum did a good deal

of investing too," Kaylee said. "Ostensibly to help people who didn't have the money to get up and running by themselves."

"Those were the good PR opportunities. But evidently he was quite a shark." Mary trimmed stems and tucked the roses into the vase.

Kaylee admired how steady Mary's hands were as she worked, despite the subject matter. "A shark how?" she asked.

"From what Maddox gleaned, Mitchum wanted to expand his reach from owning most of the Seattle market to most of the state of Washington market and maybe even beyond that," Mary explained.

"How did the other funeral home owners feel about him?"

"Many of them spoke about him with a mixture of disgust and awe."

"Meaning the ones who didn't feel targeted by him had more respect while the others were afraid of him?" Kaylee asked.

"Basically, yes. They all agreed Mitchum was ruthless, and he did some good things like investing in younger people's attempts to buy their own places just to balance it out. Although those people ended up owing him, so he basically owned whatever businesses they had too."

"I was afraid of that."

"Mitchum also wanted to have a location on Orcas Island," Mary went on. "This is a lovely—and prestigious—place."

Kaylee frowned. "He wanted to expand here? But how many funeral homes can one little island have? I mean, Giles and Nathan have most of the area covered."

"Exactly," Mary said.

"Wait. Mitchum was trying to buy them out?" Kaylee's head spun.

Mary hesitated. "The sheriff didn't get a straight answer on that. But island funeral establishments are especially attractive, because they have a guaranteed clientele. Christopher told Maddox that Mitchum had a whole business plan about where he wanted to expand over the next two years."

"And this was one of the places?"

"Yes."

"Giles would never sell his business," Kaylee said. "It's his life. People trust him here, and he takes pride in that."

"I know. Giles inherited the business from his father, and he wants Jay to continue the tradition. I'm not sure Jay's heart is in it, but that's another story, as you already know."

"Did Mitchum ever have a conversation with Giles about selling?" Kaylee asked.

"I have no idea," Mary said. "Maddox didn't say anything about it. I wondered myself, but the subject seemed to be off-limits."

Kaylee pondered that. "How do you think Giles would react?"

"Knowing Giles, he would probably tell Mitchum that he wasn't interested and leave it at that."

"But would Mitchum let it go?" Kaylee asked.

"It doesn't seem likely, given his usual manner of dealing with things," Mary said.

"Did the sheriff say anything about Nathan? Was Mitchum trying to buy him out too?" Kaylee kept coming back to Nathan. She was even more suspicious of him since he'd lied to her about how he'd met Seamus.

"Well, Maddox mentioned that he thought there was more to that relationship than initially met the eye," Mary said. She chose some baby's breath and added it to her arrangement, then stepped back and regarded it. "What do you think?"

"It's beautiful, but maybe some fern leaves," Kaylee replied. "Who's it for?"

"Thelma. She's so sad right now."

"That's really thoughtful." Kaylee felt terrible for Jay's mother, who didn't know where her troubled son was.

Mary tied a bow around the vase. "I wanted to do something to cheer her up."

"Did the sheriff elaborate on why he thought there was more to the relationship between Nathan and Mitchum?" Kaylee pressed. "By the way, I can't believe the sheriff gives you so much information. It's like pulling teeth when I try to talk to him."

Mary smiled. "Don't take it personally. He still sees me as an extension of the department. And we used to talk through a lot of cases. Old habits die hard."

"Well, I'm glad," Kaylee said.

"To answer your question, Maddox didn't elaborate. But I think he's still trying to work that part out without raising too much suspicion."

"Makes sense," Kaylee said. "I wish I'd had more of a chance to talk to Nathan last night. Maybe I could have found something else out."

Mary shook her head. "If Nathan really had something to do with any of this, he's on guard. He's not about to open up to you."

"True."

"It's not just Nathan who's interesting to Maddox," Mary continued.

"Did he find out anything else about Seamus?"

"No. But he did get an earful about Mitchum's son."

"Like what?"

"There was a very public falling-out between father and son a couple of years ago," Mary answered. "Christopher made a bad deal and lost a chunk of change. Mitchum reached the end of his patience and bawled him out in public. He made no secret about banishing Christopher to a permanent position running this other funeral home that was basically self-sufficient."

Kaylee let out a low whistle. Giles had been right. "How did

Christopher feel about that?"

"Apparently, he was very resentful," Mary said. "Rumors abounded that he was going to walk away, but then he changed his mind."

The plot thickened. What if ever since then Christopher had been planning his revenge while hiding behind a disinterested facade?

It was horrifying to imagine one's own child could have the propensity for that kind of violence, but blood wasn't always as thick as people wanted to believe.

Mary watched Kaylee. "I know what you're thinking, and you need to be very careful. Don't tell anyone you're checking into this. It's a volatile situation. And if the wrong person hears about it, they could come after you next."

Kaylee thought about the light in the woods behind her house last night. Had she been letting her imagination run away with her? Someone had probably been taking an innocent walk in the woods, and she'd freaked out over nothing.

Or had she? Bear had been as upset as she was.

"I don't think I can stop trying," Kaylee said. "Jay still hasn't shown up yet, and every minute he stays away, the police are getting more suspicious of him. We owe it to the Akins to help clear his name. Just because Christopher has a lot of money and contacts—I'm presuming, anyway—it doesn't mean he should be immune."

"I don't think he's immune," Mary said. "But Maddox specifically asked us to stay out of it. He's handling it."

"Does that mean you agreed?" Kaylee asked, horrified.

Mary laughed. "Do you even know me? I danced around it without really committing, of course. But I'm not sure what to do next."

"We have our garden club meeting tonight. We're going to The Ideal Meal, and the funeral convention will be there too. I think we should strike up a conversation with them."

"And what? Ask them if Mitchum was staging a hostile takeover of anyone's livelihood?" Mary said. "Or ask them if Nathan had a reason to kill Mitchum?"

"It depends on who we end up chatting with. We're all a lot prettier than Sheriff Maddox." Kaylee winked. "Let's wait and see where it goes. Hopefully an opportunity will present itself."

"You're crazy," Mary said, but Kaylee could see the wheels turning in her head.

"That's why I fit in so well here. We need to solve this mystery and clear Jay's name," Kaylee said. "Jess and DeeDee are on board. With the four of us working together, we'll figure it out. We always do."

"I guess we could see what we can find out," Mary said. "Since we are going to dinner, after all."

Kaylee laughed. "That's the spirit."

But not even laughter could dispel her jitters. She felt like things were heating up, but nothing was clearer, even with the confirmation that Christopher had a reason to be furious with his father.

Being taken down a few notches in front of everyone in the business, then feeling like he had to stay there because he had no other choice?

That sounded like motive for murder if she'd ever heard one.

13

It was time to open The Flower Patch and get this day in gear, so Kaylee pushed aside her thoughts and worries about the murder investigation. Now that they had a plan for this evening, she wanted to get everything else over with.

Their first customers were already peering through the front windows.

Kaylee hurried over and opened the shop door, flipping the sign around to *Open*. "Good morning! Come on in," she said, holding the door open wide.

Mrs. Anderson, one of Kaylee's regular customers, was the first one through the door.

She was followed by a middle-aged man, who nodded at Kaylee, then went over to the cooler and browsed the premade arrangements.

"My goodness," Mrs. Anderson said. "I was getting worried about you when you didn't unlock the door."

"That's kind of you, but there's nothing to worry about," Kaylee said. "I'm sorry to keep you waiting. What can I do for you today?"

"I want something for my guest room," Mrs. Anderson said. "I have a friend coming to stay, and it needs to be bright and welcoming."

"We have some gorgeous yellow roses right now," Kaylee said, ushering the woman over to one of the coolers. "I could add some other blooms to make it more interesting."

Mrs. Anderson inspected the flowers Kaylee showed her. She didn't seem all that impressed.

Kaylee was used to this. Mrs. Anderson stopped in often and took her flowers very seriously, which Kaylee could appreciate. However, her pickiness could wear on one's last nerve. Especially if one's nerves were already frayed.

"Roses seem too serious," Mrs. Anderson declared.

"Got it." Kaylee walked to a bucket holding some daisies. "How about these?"

Mrs. Anderson brightened. "Now those are much better."

Relieved, Kaylee made up a large bouquet for her and sent her on her way. Mary still hadn't come out of the workroom, so she headed over to her other customer, pasting on an apologetic smile. "I'm sorry for the delay. How can I help you today?"

"Giles said there was a nice shop in town that could provide flowers, so here I am," the man said. He was well-dressed in a suit, which almost hid the fact that he was portly with thinning hair.

"Are you here for the funeral convention?" Kaylee asked.

"Yes. I'm Nolan, by the way." He held out his hand.

She shook it. "It's nice to meet you. I'm Kaylee Bleu." She motioned to the cooler he'd been browsing. "What did you have in mind?"

"I need flowers for a funeral service," Nolan said. "One of my colleagues died. It's a shame."

"I'm so sorry," she said.

Nolan pointed at one of the arrangements, a subdued choice with *Lilium candidum*—white Madonna lilies—as the focal point. "I'd like this one, please."

"Nice selection." Kaylee opened the cooler door and removed the arrangement, then carried the flowers to the cash register.

Nolan followed her to the counter and reached into his pocket for his wallet. "Actually, I need to buy a few of these on a corporate account, but this one's personal."

Kaylee nodded. "Is this for Mitchum Landsdowne?" she

asked, trying to keep her voice steady.

The man regarded her curiously. "Yeah. How did you know?"

Clearly, he didn't know how small towns worked. He was probably from Seattle. "I did the flowers for your opening party," she said. "What an unexpected tragedy."

"Yes, especially since now the cops are saying someone offed him," Nolan said.

Kaylee winced at the choice of words. She could hear the undercurrent of excitement in his voice. Apparently, everyone loved a mystery. A murder was much more interesting than a heart attack or a stroke. Instead of commenting, she concentrated on ringing up the arrangement.

He handed her cash. "Anyway, we're holding a memorial service for him tonight after dinner. Before his son takes his body home."

Kaylee frowned as she gave him the change. Mary had just said the sheriff was trying to stall releasing the body. Maybe he'd run out of time. "That seems fast." She quickly added, "I mean, given what you just said about a possible murder investigation."

"Guess they did what they had to do," Nolan said. "Sometimes these things happen in the mortuary business. And Mitchum's son isn't interested in staying for the rest of the convention. Not that I'd expect him to under the circumstances, but he is a little incompetent, so he could probably use a few classes." He made a face. "I probably shouldn't say that."

Kaylee changed the subject. "Did you say you needed more flowers?"

"Yes, can you send over a few other arrangements?" Nolan asked. "We want it to look nice in there. Last respects and all. Mitchum was a good guy." He winked. "Well, as long as you were on his good side."

After Kaylee helped Nolan pick out the rest of the arrangements for the memorial, she rang up the sale and promised him they'd be delivered later that day.

As soon as Nolan walked out the door, Mary reappeared and said, "Well, that's an interesting development."

"Were you eavesdropping?" Kaylee teased.

"I couldn't help but overhear," Mary said. "I can't believe they're holding a memorial service tonight. I guess Maddox ran out of reasons to hold on to the body."

"Or he's getting pressure," Kaylee suggested. "It would make sense, if he's poking around Christopher and Christopher actually has something to hide."

They had to act fast to find out if Christopher was involved in his father's death. Once the body was released, Christopher would be gone, and they'd never get another chance to talk to him.

Kaylee's mind raced. "We should go and pay our respects this evening. It's a perfect plan B, especially if our dinner doesn't pan out. What do you think?"

Mary shrugged. "Why not?"

"Then it's a plan. Now let's see what's on our agenda for today." Taking a few deep breaths, Kaylee went behind the counter and grabbed a notebook. It always helped her to write down the major tasks for the day and how much time she anticipated each would take. Then they could schedule how to get them done.

She pulled out her order list and perused it. "So we have the flowers for the Bakers' rehearsal dinner, but those don't need to be done until Friday."

"Don't forget the library event," Mary said. "It's a little more time-consuming."

It was a dinner for the board of directors. Kaylee hadn't even started planning for it yet, and the event was this weekend already.

"Tomorrow is the farmers market," Kaylee said. The market was held at the public sculpture park, and the organizers had asked for some decorations. That would be a quick job, and she could refrigerate the flowers overnight. She wrote that down and noted an hour next to the task.

"Now we also have the memorial service flowers," Mary said. "I can work on those first, since they need to be done today."

"Great. Thank you."

"I'll get started. Let me know if you need me." Mary returned to the workroom.

When Mary was gone, Kaylee skimmed her list. She had an anniversary bouquet of roses someone had ordered for pickup today at four. Nothing else was urgent unless she got a call, so she added fifteen minutes next to that item on her list. They could get a head start on a few of the other orders that were pending.

She added another note to the list. *Find out if Mitchum was pressuring Nathan to try to sell his funeral home.*

As she reread the note, she tapped her pen against her lower lip. It would be easier said than done. Nathan wouldn't be broadcasting it, and from what Mary had told her, it didn't sound like Giles knew. So she had to figure out another way to get the information.

Kaylee hesitated, then jotted down, *Deliver flowers for memorial service.*

She could call Seamus to deliver the flowers, but what if he was involved in the murder? He may have even left town at this point, unless the sheriff had forbidden him to.

All things considered, it would be just as easy—and possibly more productive, if she managed to ask the right questions—if she handled the delivery herself.

The bell jingled over the door, and Bear barked.

Kaylee glanced over as Reese stepped into the shop.

Bear jumped up from his spot next to the cash register and hurried over to see him.

Reese reached down and petted the little dog.

"Hey," she said, smiling.

"Hi." Reese regarded her somewhat somberly. "I came to check on you and see how you're doing with . . . everything. I've been hearing a lot of concerning things. Are you all right?"

She nodded. "It's been a long couple of days, but I'm surviving."

"Good," he said. "But the whole situation is troubling. I heard that Seamus has been questioned."

Kaylee hadn't realized Reese was privy to so much of the island gossip. She'd always thought he'd stayed away from it as much as possible. But this was such big news, she guessed he couldn't help but hear things. After all, the whole town was talking about it.

"Yes, the sheriff questioned him, but it's complicated." Kaylee didn't know how much she should say. Mostly because she was still trying to understand it herself.

"I also heard that Jay's missing and they're keen to find him," Reese said.

"I didn't know that you had such a good network of information," Kaylee said, only half teasing. "Where on earth did you hear all this?"

"At the last job I did," Reese said. "One of the guys heard about it because he's friends with Giles. I guess he was there when Maddox was asking about Jay."

Kaylee sighed, feeling defeated. "I'm worried about Jay," she admitted.

"I am too, and I understand how you feel," Reese said. "But try not to let it get to you. There could be some things going on that you don't know about. Let Maddox worry about Jay."

"You're right, but I keep hearing that Jay was having some issues."

Reese cocked his head. "What kind of issues?"

"He was shirking responsibility at the funeral home, and

he got into a fight."

"That doesn't sound like him," Reese said. "Does anyone know what's going on with him?"

"Not that I've heard. What if he's in some kind of trouble? Shouldn't we be trying to help him instead of blaming him?"

"I'm sure the sheriff isn't making any assumptions. If he finds Jay, you can count on him being completely fair with him."

"I thought I heard your voice," Mary said to Reese as she came out of the workroom. "Good morning."

"How's it going today?" Reese asked.

"It's going," Mary answered. "I think it's the same for everyone right now."

Reese nodded. "There's definitely a strange vibe on the island this week. It's very unsettling." He turned to Kaylee. "I need to get to work. Walk me out?"

She nodded and followed him outside to his truck.

He leaned against it and folded his arms across his chest. "I'm sure you had a stressful day yesterday. Next time that happens, feel free to call me and talk it over if you need to."

"Thank you. That's very kind. It was such a whirlwind of a day, and I didn't want to bother you. I didn't know how late you'd be working."

Reese grinned. "The nice thing about working for myself is that I can answer the phone whenever I want. I'm always around if you need anything, okay?"

Kaylee beamed at him. She was lucky to have such considerate and caring friends. "Speaking of needing things, I do need you to take a look at a window when you get a chance. It's shutting weird."

Reese chuckled. "Boy, did I walk into that one. Here or at the cottage?"

"Here."

"I'll add it to my list. And I mean it about Jay. Let this play out. You don't need to help the process. I know how invested you get in things."

"I can't help it," Kaylee said. "He's my friend."

"I know you care about your friends and want to help Jay. But it sounds like Jay could be in some kind of trouble. He was at the scene of a murder. And no matter how good people are most of the time, they can get dangerous when they're desperate." He raised an eyebrow at her. "I really wish you'd be careful."

"I'm always careful."

"I'm serious, Kaylee."

She met his gaze squarely. "So am I. Don't worry. I have you and the sheriff on speed dial if I get in over my head."

He glanced at his watch. "I have to go. Can we reschedule a dinner out sometime? O'Brien's still sounds good to me."

"I'd like that," she said. "Text me later and let me know when you're free."

"Will do. Call me if you need anything," he said, climbing into his truck.

"I will." Kaylee waved goodbye. As she turned, she spotted Jocko McGee approaching. Fury swamped her, and she stomped over to him and jabbed a finger in his chest. "You've got some nerve showing up here after that ridiculous article this morning. How could you write those awful things about Jay?"

Jocko didn't seem the least bit intimidated by her. He even went so far as to grin at her. "No one would talk to me. I figured if they thought he was innocent, they'd say so. But no one wanted to say anything, and I had a deadline to meet." He took out his notepad and a pen. "I'd be happy to interview you now and print a retraction. We could probably even make a special edition."

"You're unbelievable," Kaylee snapped. "I already told you that it's inappropriate for me to comment. You'll have to get all your information from the sheriff's department. By the way, our sheriff doesn't take published rumors lightly. He'll have your hide for that article. I'd avoid him if I were you." She spun on her heel and stalked back into the shop.

Fortunately, he didn't follow her.

"Is everything okay?" Mary asked.

Kaylee nodded. "Just turning away a rather persistent reporter. I have to give it to Jocko—he has tenacity in spades."

Mary snorted. "I can't believe he came back. From what you told me about his last visit, you made it perfectly clear that you wouldn't be talking to him." A sparkle came into her eyes. "What did Reese want?"

"Nothing. He just stopped by to see how I was."

"Well, that was very thoughtful," Mary said with a smile. "He's a wonderful man."

Kaylee didn't know how to respond, so she retreated to the design studio on the second floor.

Bear followed her upstairs, but he detoured into her office.

She assumed he was going to take a nap in his bed, but then she heard a scratching noise. When she went to investigate, she found him pawing the filing cabinet where she kept a stash of his treats.

Bear turned to her and wagged his tail.

"Subtlety is not exactly your strong suit." Kaylee laughed as she opened the cabinet and retrieved a dog biscuit.

Bear accepted it, then carried it over to his bed in the corner and plopped down on it.

Kaylee returned to the design studio and set to work. But flowers couldn't keep her mind off everything, no matter how much she tried to focus on the task at hand. She finally gave in and called Giles.

He answered on the first ring.

"How are you?" she asked.

"I'm fine," Giles said. But he didn't sound fine. He sounded exhausted and down. Kaylee figured it would be pointless to ask if he'd heard from Jay.

"I have a couple of questions for you," Kaylee said. "I know you told me about Mitchum trying to take over as many businesses as he could. Do you know if that included Nathan's?" She held her breath, waiting for his reply.

Giles didn't respond right away, but she couldn't tell if he was completely surprised by the question.

"Why do you ask?" Giles finally said.

"I don't know. I'm concerned about Nathan."

"Why are you concerned about Nathan?"

"I saw Nathan and Seamus McCreary together," Kaylee said.

Another pause. Then, "You did?" Giles sounded puzzled.

"Yesterday I saw Seamus drop Nathan off at the inn, but allegedly Seamus is new to town and doesn't know anyone. Or so he told the sheriff."

"That's odd," Giles said.

"Nathan also lied to me about where he met Seamus when I asked him about it. He said he'd met him when Seamus did a delivery to your place on a Sunday. I guess he doesn't know that I don't make deliveries on that day."

Giles sucked in a breath.

"Was Nathan with you all day Monday?" Kaylee asked.

"No, not the entire day," Giles replied.

"Do you know where he was when he was off on his own?" Kaylee persisted.

"I didn't keep track of his whereabouts. He had his own arrangements to make for the convention, and he was doing them mostly to help me."

"So he could have been with Mitchum at some point," Kaylee

said, hating herself for making a man doubt an old friend. But Giles had a right to know her suspicions, especially if they might keep him safe later.

"I guess he could have been," Giles conceded.

"Let's go back to my question," Kaylee said. "Do you think Mitchum was trying to buy Nathan out?"

"I honestly don't know," Giles admitted. "If he was, Nathan never mentioned it to me. Also, knowing Mitchum's preferences, I'm not sure he'd be interested in Nathan's place, even as nice as it is."

"Why not?"

"It's pretty small. Nathan doesn't do a lot of the burial jobs, which quite frankly are more expensive. It's more cremation customers. Don't get me wrong. Nathan's business makes a nice living for him, but a person like Mitchum would consider it small potatoes."

"What kind of places was Mitchum interested in?"

"Mainly well-established ones. He'd already done his fair share of investing in smaller funeral homes. He could afford to go after only the best. Like the deal he's doing in Portland. It's his first out-of-state expansion, and it's a pretty big one."

Even though Kaylee had asked Giles this question before, she felt compelled to ask him again. "Did he ever approach you?"

Giles hesitated.

"Oh no," Kaylee breathed.

"It doesn't matter. He asked me several times, but he knew it was no good. I'd never sell to him or anyone. But as I said, I have no idea if he was interested in Nathan's place. Nathan never confided in me."

"That's interesting. Nathan was really eager to tell me last night about all of Jay's troubles and how Jay was confiding in him."

"He said what?" Giles said, indignant. "My son doesn't

even like Nathan. How dare he try to act like he was some kind of mentor to Jay!"

"Whatever you do, please don't mention this to Nathan," Kaylee warned. "I just wanted to get an idea of whether any of it was true, and it doesn't sound like it is."

"Of course it isn't," Giles snapped.

Giles seemed worked up, and Kaylee tried to turn the conversation back to his son. "When did you last see Jay?"

"Early on Monday," Giles answered. All the anger had faded from his voice. "And I wasn't much help. I sent him over to the park in the first place."

"You can't blame yourself. You couldn't know what would happen," Kaylee said gently. "Do you have any idea who last saw Jay?"

"No. I wish I did. Then maybe we'd actually have a solid lead on where he is." Giles sighed. "I need to let you go. I have a lot to do."

"I understand. Thanks for talking to me." She hung up, swallowing against the bad feeling in her chest. Mitchum had approached Giles at some point. Should that be concerning?

Why was Nathan telling all these lies? Especially the ones about Jay?

Was he trying to frame Jay for something he'd done?

14

Kaylee spent the rest of the day on autopilot. She and Mary were too busy to speak much. They greeted their steady stream of customers, and Kaylee was thankful Bear was there to be social since she wasn't in the mood.

Time passed quickly as she filled orders, made recommendations, and rang up sales. One man wanted a bouquet for his wife because she was mad at him, a young woman needed flowers to take to her grandmother at the nursing home, and a mother needed a bouquet for her son and daughter-in-law's new baby.

When the last customer was gone, Mary tidied up the counter and gathered her things. "I'm heading home to change for dinner."

"I'll pick you up at seven," Kaylee told her.

After Mary left, she locked the door with great relief, hooked Bear's leash on, and collected the flower arrangements Nolan had ordered. She had to deliver the flowers to Giles's funeral chapel before she could go home and get ready for dinner. While she was there, she hoped to find something out.

She loaded Bear and the flowers into her car, then drove the short distance to Giles's place.

As soon as Kaylee arrived, she noticed a lot of activity out front. Thankfully none of it was police activity. Cars were parked up and down the street in front of the building, and men in suits milled around the driveway, talking.

Kaylee pulled up as close as she could and got out of the car, leaving the back windows cracked for Bear. She retrieved the largest arrangement. It would take several trips to get all the flowers inside.

Nolan appeared at her side. "Hi again. Need some help?"

"Thank you. That would be great," she said with relief. "The rest of the flowers are in the car." She pointed to it. "Please don't let my dog out."

"No problem." Nolan hustled over to her car.

She slipped into the building through a side entrance. "Giles?" she called. "It's Kaylee."

No answer.

She peered over the top of the flowers as she walked inside the funeral chapel. One of the viewing rooms was set up with chairs, so that must be where the service was to be held. She glanced around the room. It was strange that Giles wasn't in there making sure everything was just so, but maybe he was taking care of last-minute details in his office.

On her way to his office, she almost bumped into Nathan.

"Oh, sorry," Nathan said. "I'm glad you're here. I have something for you. Follow me."

Kaylee swallowed against the panic that rose in her throat. Did she want to follow Nathan anywhere?

She took a deep breath and chided herself for overreacting. Besides, there were people all over the building and Nolan would be bringing in flowers any minute.

Nathan led her into the office.

Kaylee set the flowers down on the desk and scanned the room. "Where's Giles?"

"He's not here. He's getting a few things ready for tonight," Nathan answered vaguely. He grabbed an envelope off the desk and handed it to her.

She glanced at it, then at him. "What's this?"

"Your payment for the other day. Giles asked me to run it over to you, but I never got a chance."

"I told him not to worry about it."

"Take it," Nathan urged. "He feels awful for dropping such a big project on you at the last minute like that. It wasn't your fault the dinner had to be canceled."

"Thank you." She pocketed the envelope, trying to ignore the weird feeling she had about it.

"Do you need a place to put the flowers?" Nathan asked, gesturing to the arrangement she'd placed on the desk.

She nodded. "Nolan is bringing more in."

"Come on." Nathan grabbed the flowers and led her back into the viewing room.

When they walked to the front of the room, Kaylee noticed that someone had set up a portrait of Mitchum in lieu of a casket. She wondered if Christopher was planning to leave right after the service tonight. Would they have another service in his hometown? Would they cremate Mitchum or bury him?

She shivered. She couldn't imagine how someone could deal with death and its arrangements all day, every day. She could barely handle thinking about them for one man.

"We can set the larger arrangements up here." Nathan put the flowers down and motioned to the remaining empty spots around the portrait. "Since this is the focal point of the room."

Nolan came in balancing more of the flower arrangements.

"I'm sorry," Kaylee told Nolan. "I certainly didn't mean to make you carry all of them in by yourself."

Nolan set down the flowers, then flashed a smile at Kaylee. "It's no problem. I've gotten to admire them up close and personal. They smell amazing. There's only one left, so you can stay here and start setting up if you want. Your dog's fine, by the way," he added.

"Good," Kaylee said. "Thanks for your help."

She waited until Nolan left, then began placing the flowers, fussing with them more than she really needed to as she weighed her options. Should she try to strike up a conversation with Nathan? Talking about Seamus probably wouldn't get her anywhere. She didn't want to hear any more of his lies about Jay either.

But maybe if she brought up Mitchum's son, Nathan might be encouraged to talk, especially if he was trying to make sure someone else got blamed for this murder.

Kaylee finished placing the last arrangement, then turned to Nathan. "Do you have a minute? I want to ask you something."

Nathan had been tapping on his phone, but he paused and met her gaze. "Sure. What's up?"

"Do you know anything about Mitchum's son?"

"Just from being in the business together," Nathan answered. "What do you want to know?"

Kaylee moved closer in case anyone was lingering near the door. Nolan would be back any second with the rest of the flowers. "In light of everything that's happened this week, I can't help but be curious. I read somewhere that Mitchum and Christopher had a public disagreement and Christopher wasn't really respected or trusted by his father."

"You read that?" Nathan sounded amused. "That must have been quite an article."

Kaylee flushed a little. "I kind of inferred some things. Anyway, it sounded like a humiliating experience. I mean, I couldn't imagine one of my parents doing that to me and then continuing to work in the same industry."

Nathan shrugged. "I heard something about it. Christopher messed up and made a bad investment. I guess he got overconfident."

"What was the investment?"

"He bought a loser property," Nathan answered, "and it cost Mitchum a good deal of money to right the ship. So Mitchum humiliated Christopher in public."

"But they're family," Kaylee said.

"Hey, I don't know what to tell you," Nathan said. "I didn't say I agreed with it."

"How did Christopher feel about it?" Kaylee persisted.

"I heard he was resentful about it for a while, but obviously he worked it out with his father." Nathan cocked his head. "Why are you so interested in this, anyway?"

"Because I'm worried about Jay," Kaylee said evenly. "I'm not buying into the whole theory that he was troubled. From everything I've been hearing, I feel like there are other people with much stronger reasons to want Mitchum dead."

There. She'd said it. She held her breath, waiting for the fallout and listening for the sound of anyone nearby in case Nathan lost it on her. Was he really capable of murder? Or had she jumped to conclusions?

She couldn't read his expression, but he was watching her intently. So intently that she started to feel exposed.

Finally, after what seemed like an hour but was probably only a moment or two, Nathan said, "Jay's lucky to have a friend as loyal as you. Look, I don't want to believe it either. Jay's a good guy. But if he's innocent, where is he?"

"Maybe he's hurt," Kaylee shot back. "Maybe something happened to him. Maybe he bumped into Mitchum's killer and the person tried to hurt him too. Has anyone thought of that?"

"Of course people have," Nathan said. "Everyone's initial thought was for Jay's safety. But that doesn't change the fact that he's still missing."

"Hey, Nathan!" someone called.

Kaylee nearly jumped out of her skin. She whirled around to see Nolan watching them curiously. He held the last arrangement.

"We're getting ready to head out for drinks before dinner," Nolan said. "Are you coming?"

"I'll be right there," Nathan told him, then glanced at Kaylee.

"I should get going. We have a dinner tonight."

"I heard," Kaylee said, attempting to sound casual as she took the arrangement from Nolan and set it in place. "My friends and I are going to dinner at The Ideal Meal. We need to blow off some steam. It's been a long week for everyone."

"Really? Well, that's good." Nathan smiled. "We'll probably see you there. That's where we're going."

"Oh, how funny," Kaylee said. "Then I guess I'll see you in a little while."

"I guess so," Nathan replied impassively.

She could feel him watching as she walked out of the room. As she passed Nolan, she said, "Thanks again for your help."

"No problem. See you later."

Kaylee walked slowly back to her car. Something about Nathan's attitude was bugging her. Especially after learning from Giles that Jay didn't even like Nathan.

She thought about what Giles had said. Nathan's place not being attractive to Mitchum could be a good or bad thing, she realized. If Nathan wanted to expand and couldn't, maybe he'd wanted help—help Mitchum wouldn't have been willing to give if he didn't see Nathan's business as a potential moneymaker.

If Mitchum had wanted to buy Giles's funeral home, but not Nathan's, Nathan could have been resentful either way.

Had Jay known that Mitchum wanted his dad's place? Even if it was a half-hearted effort? Had that knowledge upset him?

Kaylee felt sad for Jay. She wished he'd trusted her enough to confide in her. Granted, many of their conversations had taken place while jogging in the park, but still, she'd felt they'd bonded.

Would they have become friends at all if Kaylee hadn't seen Jay most days in the park? She doubted it. Perhaps it was her own fault, and she should have made more of an effort. It sounded like he'd been in desperate need of a friend lately, one he could have confided in.

One who would have known him well enough to have a good guess as to where he might be hiding.

So where was he? Had something happened to him?

Kaylee climbed in her car and locked the doors, then glanced over her shoulder at Bear.

The dog sat patiently in the back seat watching her.

"What a week," she murmured. "I really hope all this ugliness gets hashed out soon. It's getting really hard to take."

Bear yipped as if he agreed.

Kaylee started toward home, but at the last minute she took a detour and headed toward the water. It might be a ridiculous idea, but she didn't feel like she had another choice.

She had to know who Seamus McCreary really was and why he was here.

She'd been focusing on Nathan and Christopher, but if Seamus knew Nathan, then she didn't want to overlook his piece of the puzzle. She wasn't sure how far she would get, but she had to try.

When she pulled up in front of Clay Tucker's cottage, she wasn't sure if she was disappointed or not that Seamus's red Prius wasn't there.

Clay was sitting outside with a torn fishing net over his knees. His hands flew as he mended the hole. He barely glanced up when she got out of the car. "If I had known everyone and their brother would be visiting me this week, I would have cleaned the place up. What can I do for you?"

"Sorry to drop in unannounced," Kaylee said. "But I have to ask you about Seamus. I'm really struggling with the fact that he's been working for me and the sheriff questioned him for murder."

Clay sighed and set his work aside. "Try to do a good deed," he muttered. "Listen, I'm not sure why Seamus has the heat on him, other than being in the wrong place at the wrong time."

"Why is he in town?"

"He's staying with me for the summer. Said he lost his job and needed a break from his life, wanted to get some peace and quiet to rethink things. Since he's a relative, I said sure. I didn't think it would be much trouble." Clay grimaced. "Guess I was wrong."

"Did he have a reason for wanting to be in Turtle Cove as opposed to somewhere else?" Kaylee asked.

"I'm not much of a gossip, as you know," Clay said.

I don't know that of anyone in this town. Kaylee held her tongue and waited for him to go on.

"He did mention hoping to connect with some old friends while he was here."

Kaylee's heart skipped. "Old friends? Like who?"

"I don't know. I never asked."

Kaylee wanted to scream in frustration. "Did you tell Sheriff Maddox that?"

"He never asked," Clay said.

"I told him," someone said from behind Kaylee.

She turned and saw Seamus walking toward them. Kaylee didn't notice his car anywhere and wondered where he'd come from. He must have parked it behind the shed. "Hi," she said, trying to keep her voice from shaking. "I wanted to come by and see you, but you weren't here."

"I'm here now." Seamus spread his hands. "I know what you're wondering. What everyone is wondering: if I poisoned that man."

"That's not—" Kaylee began.

"I'll admit I had an ulterior motive for coming here," Seamus said, interrupting her.

"You did?" Kaylee asked. Now that she was about to receive the information she sought, she wasn't sure she wanted to hear it.

"I was familiar with Mitchum Landsdowne," Seamus admitted. "My father owned a funeral home outside of Seattle."

Kaylee's mouth dropped open. "Really?"

"My parents were divorced, and my dad went in on that business venture later in life with a friend of his," Seamus explained. "He said he wanted to make it work so he could leave me something. But his friend died, and my dad couldn't keep it going on his own. So he tried to find help."

"Mitchum," Kaylee guessed.

"Yes," Seamus said. "My father knew Nathan from some industry events. Nathan said Mitchum was my dad's best bet, and he introduced them. Nathan assured my dad that Mitchum would not only invest in the business but coach him so he could learn how to run it better."

"So what happened?" Kaylee asked, though she dreaded the answer.

"Mitchum invested all right," Seamus huffed. "He convinced my dad to sell to him for much less than he should have gotten for the place. Mitchum promised to keep my dad on and pay him even more than he'd made to run it, and he vowed he'd teach my dad how to manage it better. It wasn't what my dad wanted, but in the end, he didn't have a choice."

"What happened once the deal was done?" Kaylee said.

Seamus stared at the ground. "Mitchum fired my dad. A few years later, my dad died. I think the stress of everything really took its toll."

Kaylee gasped. "I'm so sorry. When did it happen?"

"About ten years ago."

"You must have been heartbroken." Kaylee couldn't imagine losing a parent.

"I was. Furious too," he said. "Wouldn't you be? But it doesn't mean I killed Mitchum."

"Why did you really come here?" Kaylee asked.

"I guess part of me wanted to confront Mitchum," Seamus replied. "I followed his escapades, and I even started my own little mission to tell people in the business about what he'd done. A cautionary tale, if you will. I'm not sure it ever worked, but I tried."

"So you found out about the convention and got in touch with Clay." Kaylee glanced at the fisherman, who'd gone back to his work and hadn't said a word the whole time.

"I swear I just wanted to talk to Mitchum." Seamus turned to Clay. "I'm sorry. I didn't want to tell you the whole ugly story."

Clay shrugged. "No skin off my nose. You're family, and you had a need. I help my family when I can."

Kaylee found it strange that Clay appeared so calm about all this. He didn't seem worried that he'd been sharing his house with a man who had arrived in town with a vendetta. "Did anyone else know you were coming?" she asked Seamus.

"I called Nathan to tell him, and he thought I should talk to Mitchum."

"Why?" Kaylee said.

"Nathan said it would be good for me to get it all off my chest," Seamus answered. "He offered to help me find the best time to catch Mitchum alone. When I told him I was delivering the flowers from your place, he said that was perfect."

"He did? Did he say why?"

"Nathan told me he could get Mitchum over to the park before everyone else so we could have some privacy," Seamus said.

Warning bells clanged so loudly in Kaylee's head that she could barely hear Seamus anymore. "Did you see Mitchum?"

"No. I went to the park with the deliveries and hung around for a little while. But Nathan and Mitchum didn't show. While I waited for them, I thought about my father and what had happened.

I started to feel stupid about wanting to confront Mitchum."

"What did you do then?" Kaylee asked.

Seamus sighed. "I guess time really does heal wounds. I realized I needed to let all that anger and resentment go or I'd always be miserable. Besides, it wasn't like Mitchum could or would do anything to make it right. He can't bring my father back. I would have come away from that conversation more frustrated than ever. What good would it have done? So I left. I had plans anyway."

"Plans?" Kaylee echoed.

"I had a date. We went to a poetry slam in Eastsound. I read my latest for it." Seamus smiled. "I've been writing a lot of poetry since I arrived. It's the ocean air, I think. Anyway, lots of people saw me there and vouched for me with the sheriff. Mostly because they all knew my date. She's a pretty active member of the community over there."

"You're off the hook," Kaylee said. She had to admit she felt relieved. She hadn't invited a killer into her shop and into her customers' businesses after all.

"I believe I am," he said with a wry smile.

Kaylee thought of something else. "What were you doing with Nathan yesterday? I saw you dropping him off at the inn."

"Yeah, he wanted to talk and see how I was feeling about what happened to Mitchum." Seamus grimaced. "He was an awful guy, but I could never wish that on anyone. I just want to move on with my life."

"I'm sorry about what happened to your father," she said, "but I'm glad to hear that you're letting go of the resentment and moving on."

"It's taken me a long time to get past it," Seamus said. "Now that the sheriff has ruled me out, I hope they find that guy soon."

Kaylee stilled. "What guy?"

"Jay Akin. Nathan said he probably did it and he had a really good reason."

Kaylee was almost too stunned to speak. "What reason would Jay have to kill him?"

"Mitchum was trying to blackmail him."

15

After her conversation with Seamus—which had stirred up as many questions as answers—Kaylee went home to drop off Bear and change.

She gave Bear a treat, then left to pick up Mary so they could meet Jessica and DeeDee at The Ideal Meal.

When Kaylee arrived, Mary was waiting out on her front porch. She wore a blue summer dress with strappy sandals.

"You look so pretty," Kaylee said, glancing down at her simple outfit of khakis, a tank top, and a light cardigan. Picking out clothes had been difficult tonight. She couldn't get her mind to work on anything except Mitchum's death and who might have been responsible for it.

"Thank you," Mary said, closing the car door behind her. "Herb bought me this dress for our trip into Seattle a few weeks ago. How was the rest of your afternoon? Did you take the flowers to the funeral home?"

Kaylee nodded. "I also had an interesting conversation with Nathan."

"You did? What did he say?"

"He told me about Mitchum's relationship with his son. I almost feel bad for Christopher and how Mitchum treated him. But then I made a pit stop." She filled Mary in on her visit to Clay's place and her ensuing conversation with Seamus.

Mary let out a breath. "I'm so glad he's in the clear."

"Me too. But why was Mitchum blackmailing Jay? Seamus didn't have the details, and I've been racking my brain about it ever since. What would Mitchum hope to achieve? I doubt

Jay had any money."

"I can't imagine he did," Mary mused. "But maybe Nathan was just telling more lies. It sounds like he's trying to get people to think differently about Jay."

"It's so frustrating." Kaylee smacked the steering wheel with the palm of her hand. "Why doesn't Maddox question Nathan? He needs to drag Nathan into the station and put him in one of those interrogation rooms."

Mary smiled. "It doesn't quite work that way. The sheriff has to be careful. He certainly doesn't want a bunch of lawyers mucking up the works this early in the investigation, so I'm sure he's taking his time and trying to do it right."

"In the meantime, what about Jay?"

"I know," Mary said. "Everyone thinks police work is fast and furious, but lots of times it's the complete opposite." Then she grinned. "But our investigation doesn't have nearly as many rules and procedures to follow as they do. What exactly is our plan tonight?"

Kaylee shrugged. She hadn't thought that far ahead. "I think we need to make a few friends and try to get some info. Especially when those guys are at the bar. They'll be more apt to talk freely if the drinks are flowing."

"What about Nathan? Do you think he's getting suspicious?"

"He knows we're going there for dinner."

"How?"

"I told him."

Mary laughed. "At least he won't be taken by surprise."

"He's no match for the four of us," Kaylee said.

It was a beautiful night in Turtle Cove, and the women rolled down their windows to soak up the fresh air. Too bad the funeral group had missed their chance to dine outside in their lovely park, but after everything that had happened, Kaylee would bet no one wanted to go there anyway. Plus, it was probably still a crime scene.

"We need to be careful," Mary said unexpectedly.

"We will be. Sheriff Maddox must know we're sticking our noses in a little, especially with everything he's told you."

"I'm not talking about Sheriff Maddox," Mary said. "I'm talking about Mitchum's network."

Kaylee frowned. "What do you mean?"

"Think about it. Mitchum couldn't have done all these deals on his own. He had people helping him with his expansion plans. You never know who he could have upset and who could have turned on him. And more than a few of them could be almost as powerful as he was. Even though Nathan and Christopher are our prime suspects right now, there could be a much wider net."

"I have to wonder if Mitchum was running a funeral home mafia operation or something," Kaylee said. "Was he sending people out to break legs and wave guns around? Because that's almost what it sounds like, given how people talk about him with a mixture of fear and respect."

"I don't know if it was like that," Mary said. "But I do know a large amount of money was at stake. That's what Maddox said. Mitchum had his fingers in a lot of pies, so who knows who was working with him? That's what I'm saying about being careful. Mitchum wouldn't have been able to do all this alone."

"Understood," Kaylee said. "But we're going to be out in public at a busy restaurant. No one from outside Turtle Cove will think twice about us asking questions. We're just being small-town friendly, right?"

"Right." Mary gave her a stern look. "And careful."

"Of course we will be. But we also need the truth," Kaylee said, pulling into the restaurant parking lot. "We found out Seamus is innocent. Hopefully tonight we'll make some more progress."

Located on Sea Cliff Avenue, The Ideal Meal restaurant was not only a local favorite but a tourist hot spot. It was the best steak and seafood place in town, and it had a great seafood buffet.

Giles, or whoever had planned the dinner, had probably chosen the restaurant partly because of the private dining room. She figured that was where their party would end up. She was hoping the convention attendees would mingle at the bar for drinks before retreating to the private room. Otherwise she had no idea how she and her friends could meet some of them.

Kaylee and Mary entered the restaurant. A few moments later, they followed the hostess to the back, where Jessica and DeeDee already had a table.

As they walked down the hall, Kaylee gazed at the framed photos of Orcas Island scenes: people climbing mountains, hiking the trails, watching orca whales leaping out of the water, walking the beaches, dining on seafood, and visiting a local winery. It set the stage for not only the restaurant as part of this lovely community but of the whole island as a gorgeous escape.

Kaylee didn't see a party of men wearing black suits yet.

She and her friends exchanged hugs and sat down.

The waitress appeared behind them. "Welcome." She passed out the menus. "Can I get you some drinks to start?"

"I'd like some hot tea, please," Jessica said promptly.

The other women agreed.

The waitress beamed. "You got it."

As soon as she left, the foursome put their heads together.

"So what's the plan?" DeeDee asked. "When are the funeral guys coming?"

"They should be here soon," Kaylee answered, glancing around. "They were getting ready to leave when I was at the funeral home."

"Why were you at the funeral home?" Jessica asked.

"I had to deliver some flowers for Mitchum's memorial service that's happening tonight. Open to the public," she added, arching an eyebrow. "Mary and I already decided that we'll be stopping by after dinner."

DeeDee grinned. "That could get interesting."

"It sure could," Kaylee said. "So listen. Let's get started. We have a lot to talk about and even more to figure out."

Kaylee and Mary took turns filling in Jessica and DeeDee on the day's developments.

"I learned about Mitchum's business practices," Mary reported. "He was basically trying to build an empire of funeral homes in the Pacific Northwest. He wanted to expand to Orcas Island."

Jessica's eyes widened. "What does that mean?"

"He was interested in acquiring Giles's place," Kaylee said, dropping her voice even lower, "but Giles wouldn't sell. Supposedly Mitchum just let it go after asking several times. But he didn't seem like the kind of guy who would take no for an answer, so it bothers me that apparently he did with Giles."

"That does sound strange," DeeDee remarked.

"Seamus said Nathan told him Mitchum was blackmailing Jay," Kaylee stated.

"What?" Jessica sat back in disbelief. "For what?"

"I don't know. But I'm wondering whether Mitchum could have been trying to get to Giles's funeral home another way." Kaylee took a breath. "But I'm also wondering about Mitchum's interest—or lack of interest—in Nathan's place."

"Wouldn't someone building an empire want all the businesses he could snatch up?" DeeDee asked.

"You'd think so," Mary chimed in.

"Wait, you said Seamus told you?" Jessica asked Kaylee. "I knew he was involved! How did you get him to talk?"

Kaylee shook her head. "It's not what you think." She related the tragic story of how Seamus knew Mitchum.

"That's terrible," DeeDee said. "I feel sorry for Seamus."

"I feel awful for suspecting him," Jessica added.

"Me too. Fortunately, it sounds like he's come to terms with everything," Kaylee said. "For his sake, I hope he really has."

The waitress sailed over with a tray. "Here we go," she chirped, setting teacups down in front of each of them, along with two teapots for the table. She stood back and clasped her hands around her tray. "Would you like to hear tonight's special?"

The women nodded.

The waitress explained it—a create-your-own surf and turf—then said she'd give them time to think about it and bustled away.

As they perused the menu, Kaylee talked to her friends more about her theory. She was so grateful to have them in her life, especially during chaotic times like these.

"Basically, our two real suspects are Nathan and Christopher," she told them. "I'm not counting Jay, since we all know he didn't do it."

They exchanged uncomfortable glances. No one wanted to comment on Jay's status right now. The longer he was gone, the more worrisome the whole situation became.

"Christopher wants to head out of town," Jessica reminded them. "Surely that's suspicious."

Kaylee nodded. "Nathan is trying to make sure Jay looks bad."

"They both had opportunity," Mary said.

"Did they both have motive?" DeeDee asked.

"Christopher definitely did," Kaylee said. "I'm not sure about Nathan. But given the fact that he was the one who referred Seamus's father to Mitchum all those years ago tells me he's got history with Mitchum. It's interesting that he acts like he doesn't. Or at least that they weren't close."

"Maybe they weren't," Jessica countered. "Maybe Nathan

just knew of Mitchum and thought he could help Seamus's father at the time."

"Maybe," Kaylee hedged.

"But?" Jessica asked.

"Nathan also had a lot to say about Christopher when I asked him," Kaylee responded. "It almost seems like he's desperate for no one to suspect him, so he'll spill juicy tidbits about everyone else, whether they're true or not."

Jessica leaned forward eagerly. "You asked him? When?"

"Earlier tonight when I went to drop off the flowers for the memorial."

"What did Nathan say?" DeeDee asked, picking up her tea. She appeared worried.

"Christopher messed up and lost all kinds of money," Kaylee explained. "Mitchum publicly humiliated him and relegated him to what he considered a foolproof post at one of his more established businesses. Not surprisingly, Christopher was resentful about it."

"I can't say I blame him for that, but was he resentful enough to murder his own father?" Jessica murmured.

Silence covered the table for a moment. How could they know?

"Do you think Christopher will step in and continue building the company as his father did?" Mary asked. "He doesn't seem like he's assertive enough to hold whatever businesses Mitchum already has, much less add more."

DeeDee shrugged. "I don't know anything about the funeral business, but it would seem that if Mitchum was trying to do deals, he had other people involved. Will everything simply stop now that he's gone, or are there people who will still benefit from the bottom line? If so, will they keep it going? Would they welcome Christopher as a new head, or would they shut him out?"

Kaylee had to admit they were great questions, but she had no idea what the answers were.

"Maybe Christopher was only useless in his father's eyes," Jessica suggested.

Kaylee thought about Jessica's comment as she sipped her tea. What if Christopher had been watching and waiting all this time? Bad graces and all, he had to be accounted for somehow in his father's estate.

Perhaps Christopher's reason for staying in the business after public humiliation was twofold: he'd been too lazy or limited to find another career, and he was biding his time to get revenge on his father, knowing he'd come into a significant inheritance when Mitchum died.

"Maybe we'll find out tonight," Kaylee said. She turned to see the hostess ushering a group of men through the room.

The attendees of the funeral directors' convention were finally here.

Kaylee caught Giles's eye as he passed. He still looked somber.

Giles nodded at them as he walked by, but he didn't pause.

Nathan was behind him. As he passed their table, he smiled at them and waved. His gaze lingered on Kaylee a moment too long.

Or maybe she only imagined it.

When they were gone, Kaylee said, "One other thing that has been bothering me. Christopher has a great motive, but he didn't seem like the type who would have that kind of knowledge of poisonous plants."

"I was thinking the same thing," Jessica said. "Plus, I can't picture him running around in the woods and gathering nightshade."

"He could have researched it online," DeeDee reasoned. "Or maybe he found someone to get it for him. Aside from us, there are plenty of people around here who take an interest in flowers and plants."

"That would mean major premeditation if Christopher asked

someone to collect the plants," Mary said. "Who would field a request like that without asking questions about it? And why wouldn't they have come forward with the information after Mitchum died? I mean, the police haven't released any official statements, but everyone knows about it by now, and you'd think someone would wonder if the deadly plant they just gave someone else could have been involved." She shook her head. "It doesn't feel right."

"Sadly, it doesn't," Kaylee admitted.

Jessica burst out laughing. "Sadly?"

Kaylee stared at her. "What?"

"It seems an odd thing to say when you realize a guy might not have killed his own father."

Kaylee flushed. "That's not what I meant. I meant it's sad that we don't seem to be any closer to figuring out who killed Mitchum than we were the day he died. I don't want anyone to be a killer. We've barely met Christopher, and I can't fathom anyone we know actually being capable of doing this."

"Doing what?"

Kaylee turned to find Deputy Nick Durham standing there with a blonde wearing a red dress. She frowned at him. "Nothing. We were just chatting."

"Really?" Nick raised an eyebrow. "I worry when the four of you are 'just chatting.' Especially with everything that's going on around here."

"Why? What's going on?" Kaylee asked, unable to resist.

Nick gave her a warning glare.

"Come on." Nick's companion tugged on his arm. "I'm starving."

"Sorry," Nick told her as he squeezed her hand. "Kaylee, try to stay out of trouble, please." With one last look at them all, he followed his date to their table.

Jessica rolled her eyes. "I wonder if he's really on a date or hoping to do some undercover investigating of the funeral crew."

"Who is Nick's date?" DeeDee asked. "I've never seen her before."

"I wonder how he keeps track of all these blondes," Jessica mused. "It must be like another full-time job."

Kaylee stifled a smile. Nick's love life was a favorite topic of conversation on the island, both within the confines of the Petal Pushers and in broader groups. He was attractive and had a well-earned reputation as a flirt.

"They're not all blonde," DeeDee remarked. "The last one was brunette."

"Why did he tell only you to stay out of trouble?" Jessica said to Kaylee. "We're all trouble."

"I think he knows that," Kaylee said drily. She glanced at Nick's table and couldn't help but notice it was near the room where the funeral directors had congregated. Maybe he was here to eavesdrop after all. But it seemed unlikely that someone would offer up a confession to colleagues on the night of his victim's memorial.

They went back to focusing on the menu.

The waitress, who had been hovering in an obvious attempt to gauge whether they were ready to order, came over to their table, pad and pen poised. Evidently, she wanted to get things moving. They were most likely booked up tonight.

Kaylee chose a light surf and turf of grilled shrimp and chicken, but her mind definitely wasn't on the food. Jessica and DeeDee engaged in a short, vigorous debate over salmon versus risotto, but eventually DeeDee chose the risotto and Jessica picked the chef's specialty crab, making them all laugh. Mary ordered a salad.

Kaylee heard her phone buzzing. She removed it from her purse and checked the screen. She didn't recognize the number, but it was local. She answered, sticking a finger in her other ear so she could hear better.

The voice kept breaking up, and she couldn't tell whether it was a man or a woman, much less what the person was trying to say.

She pulled the phone away from her ear to see how many bars she had. The service inside the restaurant was bad.

Swiftly, she stood. "Excuse me for a minute," she said to her friends.

"Where are you going? Who's calling you?" Jessica asked with a grin.

"I'll bet it's Reese," DeeDee added in a singsong voice.

Kaylee ignored their teasing. "I'll be right back. Don't eat my dinner." She hurried toward the front door.

As she pushed through the crowd in the vestibule and left the restaurant, she said breathlessly into the phone, "Hello?"

Nothing.

She glanced at the screen.

The line went dead.

16

This was ridiculous. Kaylee knew she should simply go back inside the restaurant and rejoin her friends. The call probably wasn't even for her. Even in this age of saved phone numbers and caller ID, plenty of people still called the wrong number.

But what if . . . ?

Exhaling a sigh of frustration, she redialed the number, walking around the rear of the building as she did so.

While she waited for an answer, she heard voices coming from around the corner. Kaylee paused, straining to hear. What was around there, anyway? Probably the back door of the restaurant, where the trash was. Perhaps she was hearing restaurant workers on their break.

Or perhaps not. Curiosity won out, and she inched closer to the sound of the voices. If it was someone interesting, she wanted to know.

Glancing around to make sure no one was paying attention to her as they entered and exited the restaurant, she hurried over to the wall nearest the corner and pressed herself against it, silently urging them to speak up.

"We've got to get this finished," a man said. "We've come way too far."

"Yes." The other man's voice was lower, but it sounded more controlled and authoritative. "But if plan A doesn't work, we have to find another way. Whatever it takes." His tone left no room for argument. "And that's your job."

The two voices sounded familiar, but they were too far away for her to be able to identify the speakers.

She'd bet money these men were from the funeral convention, though. What did they intend to finish? Did it have to do with Mitchum? With his death?

The voices grew louder. They must be walking while they talked. Were they about to emerge from around the corner and bust her?

Kaylee glanced around anxiously, searching for a place to hide. The only thing nearby was a column that was barely wide enough for her to fit behind. She pressed herself against the wall, stifling a bout of hysterical laughter that bubbled up in her throat. If anyone was watching her right now, they'd think she'd lost her mind.

Perhaps she had. These were probably totally innocent, random people. They might not even be from the funeral directors' convention. Maybe they were restaurant workers, talking about how to salvage a bad dinner.

She really needed to get her imagination under control.

Or maybe they were talking about doing something wrong. The restaurant was certainly full of people tonight, from both the funeral business and beyond. Any of the patrons could be talking about a shady-sounding business deal.

Or a murder.

But what a coincidence *that* would be.

Kaylee forced herself to stop jumping to conclusions. People made business deals all the time. She was reading too much into it. She was imagining murder and mayhem everywhere because of what had happened to Mitchum.

Maybe. Maybe not. She didn't believe in coincidences anymore. All she knew was that the funeral convention had come to town, a guy known for his ambitions to own every single funeral home in the area was part of it, and that guy had ended up dead. Also, another member of the funeral contingency was missing and a murder suspect.

Still, Kaylee wanted to get closer to these men. She wanted to hear more and see if she really did recognize their voices.

The men were now speaking more quietly, or they had moved away from their original spot.

Taking a deep breath, she pressed herself closer to the wall and poked her head around, keeping as much of herself behind the wall as possible.

The men were maybe fifty feet away from her, talking softly. She could no longer hear them, but she could now see the men clearly under an exterior light.

It was Nathan and Nolan.

With a gasp, she pulled her head back around the corner. "I knew I recognized their voices," she muttered quietly.

She wondered what was going on. Did Nathan and Nolan have an underhanded business deal in the works? Or had they partnered up for something even more sinister?

Things were looking worse and worse for Nathan.

But she couldn't prove it, since she didn't actually know what they were talking about. She wished she could get closer and hear them, but there was no way to do that without the men seeing her. They would both recognize her.

Maybe they'd walk this way. Or maybe she could somehow get to the back door of the restaurant and be able to listen from inside it.

Just as she realized she'd have to either make a dash for it and hope for the best or give up and go inside, the men started pacing back toward her, and she could hear their voices again.

"Listen," Nolan said, his voice growing louder as he seemed to get agitated. "I don't know what else to do here. There isn't a plan B. It wasn't supposed to go down this way. Him dying wasn't part of the plan."

"Well, I guess we can't help that now." Nathan's voice,

louder and more forceful, floated toward her. "He's dead, and we need to keep going."

Kaylee froze.

In the silence that followed, her phone rang. When had she turned the ringer up so loud? She desperately jabbed at the phone's screen, trying to decline the call.

Perhaps she should answer it. That way if Nathan and Nolan caught her, she might be able to convince them that she hadn't been eavesdropping. Or at least, if they tried to kidnap or hurt her, whoever was on the other end would hear it.

But there was still silence from around the wall, and Kaylee didn't wait around to find out what was going to happen next. She took off, only glancing behind her when she was in sight of the front door of the restaurant.

There was no one there.

Maybe they hadn't seen her after all.

Kaylee reached the door and yanked it open, stepping inside the foyer and sagging against the wall as people streamed past her, sending her curious looks. She needed to return to her table.

Glancing down at her phone, she realized it had been Reese calling. She had to laugh. Her friends would get a kick out of that when she told them.

She fired off a quick text message to Reese. *Out with the girls for dinner. Can I call you later?*

He texted back, *I'll be here. Give me a call when you can.*

She scrolled through her other calls, searching for the one that had started this little escapade in the first place. She paused at the other number. It was definitely the Orcas Island area code, but it wasn't a number she recognized.

Curious now, she hit redial and listened to it ring.

No answer. And no voice mail or anything. Just endless ringing.

She hurried back to their table, still clutching her phone. She stopped short when she saw Nathan standing there. But where was Nolan?

Nathan met her eyes, his gaze moving to the phone in her hand, then back up to her face. He smiled, but there was something in his eyes she couldn't quite read.

Kaylee swallowed, pasted on a smile, and approached.

All three of her friends looked up.

"Hey, Nathan," Kaylee said breezily as she returned to her seat.

"Hi. Having fun?" he asked. His voice sounded nothing like it had a few minutes ago.

"I am," she returned coolly. "You?"

Nathan nodded. "Nice night, huh?"

He sounded so innocuous, but she felt her blood run cold. Was he telling her he knew she'd been outside and that she'd overheard his conversation? "It sure is," she said.

"Where have you been? Was that Reese?" Jessica demanded. "We ate all the appetizers, and dinner is delicious." She held up a forkful of her crabmeat to make the point.

"Good," Kaylee said, trying to keep her voice light. "I'm starving." She picked up her fork, but it hung suspended in the air as she watched Nathan talking to Mary. It sounded innocent enough—something about how to know whether a florist had a good selection—but given her suspicions about Nathan, it somehow seemed like he was threatening her friend or even Kaylee herself.

They finished their conversation, and he strolled away.

Kaylee watched him go. She realized she had no appetite anymore.

"What's going on?" DeeDee asked, leaning over. "You look like you've seen a ghost."

"I'm fine. I'll tell you later." Kaylee pushed her food around on her plate, trying and failing to summon her appetite. But then she remembered Nick was there. She needed to fill him in. "I'll be right back."

"You're not fine," DeeDee said. "Where are you going now?"

Mary was staring at her too. She hated to worry her friends like this, but they would only be more worried if she told them the truth.

"Nowhere. I just have to ask Nick a question." Before they could press her, Kaylee rushed over to Nick's table.

Nick's date seemed less than pleased about the interruption.

"I'm sorry. I wouldn't interrupt if it wasn't important," Kaylee said to her. "Nick, can I speak to you for a minute?"

He must have seen something in her expression that piqued his interest, because he nodded. "Sure." He turned to his date. "Sorry, but will you excuse us? This will only take a minute."

Kaylee motioned for Nick to follow her and led him outside into the restaurant entryway.

"What's up?" he asked.

"How's the Landsdowne investigation going? The chief won't talk to me. It's almost like he's shutting me out," she said. "Christopher Landsdowne plans to get out of town as soon as possible, and Nathan Anghelone is acting really strangely. Are you guys anywhere near an arrest?"

"I can't talk to you about it. Now if you know something, you need to tell me, but the information sharing can't go both ways this time."

"I'm not in the mood for your teasing," Kaylee said. "This is serious."

"I'm not teasing you," he said. "The sheriff gave specific instructions that you're not to be part of this investigation."

Kaylee felt as if she'd been punched in the stomach. "What? Why? What did I do?"

"He didn't explain," Nick said, his tone distinctly remorseful.

"Have you at least been taking all the possibilities into account?" Kaylee asked. "It seems like the sheriff is focusing on Jay. I realize Jay is still missing and it seems suspicious, but you know him as well as the rest of us. You know he didn't do it."

She didn't mean to sound so harsh, but she couldn't help it. The more she heard, the more she needed to know Maddox and his team were focused on the right people. And the longer it took them, the more worried she got about Jay. Being shut out of the investigation only made matters worse.

She needed to talk to Giles again. She had a feeling he knew more about what Mitchum had been doing than he was letting on. Unfortunately, it was affecting Jay and whatever had gone on with him and Mitchum.

"This time, you need to mind your own business."

Kaylee bristled. "This whole situation has affected my business. I'm the one who found the body. When that happened, it *became* my business."

Nick sighed but didn't respond.

"Fine. I'll tell you what I know. I'm not sure if you've done your research on Mitchum, but he didn't have many friends," Kaylee said. "One of the people who knew him is acting very suspiciously, and he's practically sitting next to you tonight."

"Kaylee—" Nick began.

"No, you said you wanted to hear what I know," she said, cutting him off. Her patience had worn thin. "There are two men in that party right now who might know a lot more about your dead guy than anyone else in this town. They were just outside in the parking lot talking about some plan B and whatever it takes to get something finished. And they mentioned 'him dying' and how that hadn't been part of the original plan. I don't know about you, but I only know of one *him* who died around here recently."

"Wait. Who? When did you hear this?"

"Just now. They were out back behind the restaurant." She waved in the general direction.

"Why were *you* out back?" Nick demanded.

"I stepped outside to take a phone call. It turned out to be a wrong number. Anyway, I heard voices I recognized, including Nathan's," Kaylee said impatiently. "And he lied."

"About what?"

"How he met Seamus," she replied. "He didn't run into him while Seamus was making a delivery on a Sunday. We're not open on Sundays. Nathan knew him from a long time ago when he referred Seamus's father to Mitchum to get help for his funeral home business."

"Did you know the other guy?" Nick asked.

"Yes, he's one of the funeral directors attending the convention," Kaylee said. "I met him today when he dropped by the shop to buy flowers for Mitchum's memorial service."

"Did they see you?"

Kaylee hesitated. "Not that I know of."

Nick shook his head. "If they didn't see you, how did you see them?"

"I peeked around the wall."

He made a strangled sound. "Do you realize how easy it would have been for them to see you? And what if they are planning something sinister? What would they have done to you if they'd realized you were eavesdropping and could potentially bust them?"

"I keep telling you they didn't see me," Kaylee argued. "They probably knew I was there because my phone started ringing, and they heard it from behind the wall, but they didn't follow me or anything."

"I thought you were already on the phone," Nick said through gritted teeth.

"I said I got a call," Kaylee reminded him. "When I went

outside to take it, I still couldn't hear the person, and then the line went dead. That's when I heard them talking, so I listened. Then I got another call."

"But they didn't see you?" Nick pressed.

She shook her head. "When I came back in, Nathan was at our table. He probably guessed it was me outside."

"So if he was plotting some terrible thing, he knows you're on to him now."

"Right. That's why I'm telling you, in case I vanish or something."

"Great," Nick said. Kaylee expected him to say more, but he yanked open the door and headed back inside the restaurant.

When Kaylee made it back to the table, her three friends made no bones about the fact that they demanded a complete report on Kaylee's conversation with Nick and they wouldn't take no for an answer.

"What on earth is going on?" Jessica hissed. "And why don't we know about it?"

Kaylee glanced around to see if anyone from the funeral contingency was nearby. "That call I got? It wasn't Reese. Well, the second one was, but that doesn't matter."

"So who called you the first time?" DeeDee asked.

Kaylee gave them the rundown of her escapade outside and her subsequent conversation with Nick.

Mary paled as she talked. When Kaylee finished, Mary asked, "Do you think Nathan really killed Mitchum? I know we've been talking about it, but this seems so real."

"I don't know," Kaylee said. "Nolan specifically said someone dying wasn't part of the plan. I have no idea what the plan is, but it sounds like something went off the rails."

"If that's the case, then it means Nathan may have gone rogue," DeeDee said. "Who knows what else he might do?"

17

Kaylee was the first one who found her voice. "Surely we're making more of this than there is. It's not a movie or anything."

"I know it's not," DeeDee said. "But how many times have you found yourself in the middle of something that might as well be? You have to be careful. We don't want to see you get hurt. I'd much rather you erred on the side of caution and came off a little paranoid than throw yourself into something dangerous because you didn't believe it could be possible."

"I know. I'm sorry." Kaylee squeezed her eyes shut. It had been such a long day, and after barely sleeping the past two nights—especially last night, after the scare she'd had—she felt like she was in a complete fog. "I'm stressed right now. I wish the cops would figure it out already."

"It's okay. I get it." DeeDee touched her hand. "I don't think we're going to get to hang out with these guys at the bar, though. Nick is watching us like a hawk."

"I don't either, but don't forget the memorial service," Kaylee said. "I think we should still attend. As supportive citizens, of course."

"Right," Mary said drily. "Because everyone who knows us will believe we're solely there as supportive citizens."

"I'm not too worried about that," Kaylee said. "I just want this solved. Christopher can't be allowed to skip town if there's a chance he committed murder. Or maybe he was in on it with Nathan."

"Didn't Sheriff Maddox talk to him?" Jessica asked.

"He did," Mary said. "But I don't know what Christopher told him."

Kaylee thought of something. "You never said if the sheriff found out what Jay and Mitchum were arguing about Monday morning at the bakery. Did Maddox ask Christopher?"

Mary looked thoughtful. "I'm sure he did, but he didn't mention it to me."

"Good," Kaylee said. "A conversation starter, then. Because I'm going to ask him."

"Oh boy," Jessica said. "This is going to get interesting."

Kaylee had a feeling that *interesting* was an understatement.

After a dessert that Jessica admitted rivaled even some of her chocolate concoctions, Kaylee and Mary drove over to Akin Funeral Chapel, pulling up to the curb behind Jessica and DeeDee in Jessica's car.

The four women met on the sidewalk.

"I feel like I'm in a spy movie," Jessica whispered, her eyes bright with excitement.

"Giles is inside," DeeDee reported. "I saw him walk in when we arrived. Do you think anyone but the funeral guys will show up for the memorial?"

"We're here," Jessica pointed out.

"Yeah, but we're nosy," DeeDee said.

Kaylee had to laugh at her friend's matter-of-fact tone. "We are that. Let's go," she said.

Part of her was nervous, though. What if Nolan was here? What if he recognized her and got suspicious? Then again, Nathan had probably said something to him, so that ship might have already sailed.

She wondered if Nick would drop by. Or maybe the sheriff.

Shouldn't this be part of the investigation?

But Nick had made it clear that she wasn't welcome in the investigation. So she'd just worry about herself and her friends.

"Do you think we should wait until more people arrive?" DeeDee asked. "You know, so we blend in?"

"I don't think we're going to blend in no matter how many people arrive," Jessica said. "We might as well go in and pretend we're here to offer Giles some moral support."

"I think Giles might figure out that we're really here to be nosy," DeeDee muttered, but she followed them inside.

"Still," Kaylee said, "I think he'll appreciate it that we took the time to stop by."

Kaylee hadn't paused to take in the funeral home's effect when she'd delivered the flowers earlier. She'd forgotten the impression it gave upon arrival, and now she stopped to appreciate why Giles's place was so well received in the community. The foyer was tasteful, striking the perfect balance between elegant and welcoming that would instantly put a grieving family at ease.

A large easel in the foyer displayed a picture of Mitchum wearing a tailored charcoal-gray suit. Kaylee had set arrangements on either side of it, but now she studied the photo of a smiling Mitchum in happier days. Had he once been young, carefree, and unassuming? What had the world done to him that when his life was cut short, he had become a greedy, cruel predator of a man, who was largely feared and despised? Kaylee found herself saddened over the loss of that hopeful young man he must have been, just as much as she grieved the loss of life.

As they headed toward the viewing room, Kaylee scanned the small groups of people already gathered. The men wore dark suits, and the women were clad in various black dresses.

She glanced down at her own outfit and cringed. She was dressed much too casually for a funeral event. She wished she'd thought of that when she was getting dressed, but she'd been too preoccupied with the murder investigation. Though she hadn't liked Mitchum in the short time she'd known him, she felt everyone deserved to be respected at their last rites.

Abby stood in line to sign the guest book. Nathan wasn't with her.

Kaylee caught her friends' attention and nodded toward Abby, and the four got in line behind her.

Abby turned. "How nice to see you."

"You too. So where's Nathan?" Kaylee asked. "We bumped into him earlier at The Ideal Meal, and I thought he would be here."

"He should be here soon," Abby said, then faced DeeDee. "I'm looking forward to your class."

DeeDee smiled. "Thanks. Me too."

After Abby signed the guest book and moved away, Kaylee walked up and scanned the page. So far, only about fifteen people, mostly names she didn't recognize, had signed in. They were probably part of the funeral directors' convention. She scrawled her name, then stepped aside and handed the pen to Jessica.

When Kaylee peered into the viewing room, she breathed a sigh of relief. She didn't see Nathan or Nolan. She wasn't sure she wanted to run into them again. It was probably wishful thinking on her part, but maybe they'd decided not to come. Especially if they'd had a hand in Mitchum's fate.

"Kaylee, how good of you to come."

She turned and found Giles standing behind her. "How are you?" she asked.

He let his gaze drift around the room before answering. "I'm fine."

"It's a nice service. You always do such a great job." It sounded lame, but it was all she could come up with.

"Thank you." Giles raised an eyebrow at her. "I have to say I'm a little surprised to see you here. I thought you didn't really know Mitchum."

DeeDee coughed behind her.

Kaylee ignored her friend and gave Giles a small smile. "Can I talk to you in private for a second?"

"I really shouldn't—"

"The girls can keep an eye on things," Kaylee interrupted. "There aren't even that many people here yet. Please."

"Very well. I'm sure things will be fine for a little bit." Giles waved her friends toward the visitation room. "You can go in. The dinner is breaking up, so more people will be along shortly."

Kaylee followed him to the little room with chairs, tissues, and water off to the side of the main room.

She closed the door and spun around to face him, not even giving him a chance to take a seat. "Nathan is dirty," she stated.

He stared at her as if she'd lost her mind.

"I'm serious. I was at the dinner. I went outside, and I heard him talking to Nolan. They were discussing making their move and getting something done, whatever it took. It sounded bad."

Giles remained silent.

"Nathan said something to Seamus about Mitchum blackmailing Jay," Kaylee continued. "Will you please tell me what's really going on?"

"Blackmailing Jay?" Giles let out a strangled laugh. "I appreciate your desire to help, but I think you're reaching now. My son has nothing worth being blackmailed for."

"I'm just repeating what I've been told," Kaylee said. "And I don't think it's so far-fetched. You said before that Mitchum expressed an interest in buying your funeral home. Did it turn serious? Was he willing to go to great lengths to get it?"

Giles sank down into one of the chairs with a defeated sigh. "I don't see why it matters anymore anyway." He rubbed his face with both hands, then let them drop into his lap. "Yes, he did. He's been pursuing it very seriously the last few years. If you want to know the truth, he was starting to wear me down."

Stunned, Kaylee perched on the edge of the opposite chair. She didn't know what she'd been expecting, but it definitely wasn't this. "I thought you told him no."

He shrugged. "I did. I said no several times—for two years, actually. I inherited this business from my father, and I wanted it to become my son's. But then I thought about what it would mean to sell for a more than fair price, which was what he was offering."

Kaylee couldn't think of a thing to say in response, so she waited for him to continue.

He spread his hands wide. "Early retirement. More time to travel with my wife. The chance to enjoy life without getting calls in the middle of the night to pick up the deceased. And with Jay's lackadaisical attitude recently, I thought maybe it would be worth it to give up the fight and let him choose his own path. So I began to seriously consider it."

"Did Jay know?"

"I didn't tell anyone. Not even Thelma. And honestly, I was going back and forth almost daily on the pros and the cons of both decisions."

"So no one else knew about it?"

"I'm not sure. But I wouldn't have been surprised if Mitchum told people that he'd worn me down and that I was contemplating his offer."

"And then he was killed."

He nodded.

Kaylee sat back, pondering this revelation. "Wow," she finally said. "I thought you loved this business. I can't even imagine your funeral home being run by someone else."

"I do love the business," Giles said. "But if my son doesn't want it, or if he isn't around to run it—well, it isn't worth very much, is it?"

Kaylee felt sorry for him on many counts, but most of all for the huge questions surrounding Jay. Where was he? What had happened to him? If he'd just vanished on his own, what had driven him? Had he found out about his father's impending decision and felt responsible, so he skipped town? Or had he fled the business his father had prepared him for his whole life?

Giles seemed like he was about to say something else to her, but then he evidently changed his mind.

Kaylee waited a moment, and when it was clear he wasn't going to speak, she did. "Now what?"

He looked at her. "What do you mean?"

"Did Mitchum have business partners?" she asked. "Is there anyone else who was counting on this deal?"

Giles straightened, his expression alarmed. "Why, I have no idea. I never talked to anyone but Mitchum. He always approached it like two old friends who were simply talking." He made a face. "But I saw right through him."

"Mitchum must have been working with someone else," Kaylee said. "Or even multiple people. I'm starting to think that Nathan was one of them."

But did that mean Nathan had killed Mitchum over it? Or were there two separate things at play here—business and another motive for murder?

"I can't believe it," Giles said so quietly that Kaylee almost didn't hear him. "I can't believe any of this. If you don't mind, I'd like to be alone right now."

"Of course. Let me know if there's anything I can do for you." Kaylee walked slowly out to the main room, leaving Giles in his chair. He didn't seem to want to move. He appeared frail and older than he should, and it made her sad.

Kaylee was done playing Nancy Drew for the night, and she wanted to leave. She searched for her friends.

Jessica and DeeDee were engaged in conversation with someone in the viewing room, and it didn't look like they would be done anytime soon. Mary was nowhere in sight.

She was frustrated because she didn't see Nick or the sheriff. Apparently, nobody in the sheriff's department cared about what was going on.

Kaylee leaned against the wall in the main room, hoping to become invisible until she could slip out, and allowed her mind to wander. Something was nagging at her, but she couldn't put her finger on it.

What had Nathan and Nolan been talking about at the restaurant? Which deal? Was Giles's business a big acquisition for them? Or just one of many? Kaylee wished she knew what deal they had been talking about. And if it had to do with Mitchum's death.

She still wanted to get the scoop on Christopher, but she hadn't seen him yet tonight. That was her primary reason for being here, but she hadn't thought about what would happen if he didn't show up. Then again, it hadn't occurred to her that a man might not come to his own father's funeral.

But would it be different if he had killed his father?

Kaylee spied coffee on the other side of the room and headed toward it. Lost in her own thoughts, she poured herself a cup. As she turned to grab the creamer, she bumped into someone who'd just walked over to the coffeepot.

"I'm sorry," she said, grabbing a napkin to wipe up the spill.

"No problem."

It was Christopher.

18

Kaylee nearly dropped her coffee.

Up close, she could tell Christopher was about her age, maybe a few years younger. His blond hair was thinning, and he had a faint five-o'clock shadow. His suit was wrinkled.

She steadied her nerves, forcing her hand to stop shaking so she didn't spill coffee all over him. "Hi. I'm Kaylee Bleu," she said. "I own the local flower shop."

He finished pouring his coffee, then glanced at her. "Hello. Christopher Landsdowne."

"Yes, I recognized you," she said, hoping she sounded casual. "I saw you with your dad and Jay in the bakery a few days ago. I'm so sorry for your loss," she added.

"Thank you," Christopher said, sipping his coffee. "It's been a difficult week, and it's been even harder trying to keep up appearances, you know?"

"Yes, of course," Kaylee said. "I can't imagine. Are you here the rest of the week?"

He shook his head. "Just another way I would have disappointed him. My dad would have expected me to stay for the convention, but I'm leaving first thing in the morning. They've finally released my father's body. They were holding on to it because of the . . . circumstances."

Kaylee nodded. She could have feigned ignorance, but he had probably gathered that everyone in town knew what was going on. "It's a terrible thing," she said, watching his face closely.

"It is," Christopher agreed.

"Jay's a friend of mine," Kaylee said. "He's usually easygoing.

I couldn't help but wonder what had him so angry that morning."

He frowned at her. "Angry?"

"He and your dad got in a fight at the café, remember?"

She expected a flicker of recognition in his eyes, but there wasn't one. "Everyone was always angry at my father," he said with a wry smile. "It's hard to keep track of why."

"Oh," Kaylee said, taken aback. It was nothing she hadn't deduced herself, but it still sounded rather shocking coming from Mitchum's own son. It also surprised her that he seemed so matter-of-fact about it.

She decided to try a different tactic. "Jay's been missing since that night. I was wondering if their argument might have had something to do with what happened to your dad," she finished, hating herself. It sounded like she was accusing Jay.

But Christopher didn't appear to pick up on that. In fact, he seemed quite disengaged for someone who had recently lost his father to a murder.

He sighed. "I have no idea what happened that night," he said, running his hand through his hair. "And I honestly don't remember their argument. I tuned out most of what my father said."

Kaylee had seen that for herself, but she was surprised at his admission.

"I wasn't here Monday night," he continued. "After I left the café that morning, I had to go back and fill in at my funeral home during a service. My stand-in director got tied up and couldn't be there. So even after I heard the news, I wasn't able to return to town until nearly ten that night."

"Oh," Kaylee said, knowing it sounded lame. But what else could she say?

"I know everyone's trying to figure out who killed him," Christopher said. "But he didn't treat people very well. I hate to say it, but I think this was a long time coming."

A man came up to Christopher to offer his condolences.

Kaylee took the opportunity to slip away.

She thought about what Christopher had told her. If he was telling the truth, he hadn't even been on the island Monday night. She figured Maddox had already found that out. It would have been easy enough to prove—if Christopher had indeed been running a funeral service.

Which left only one person. One she still hadn't seen here yet. And one she wasn't sure she wanted to wait around for.

DeeDee came up behind her. "Hey," she said. "You ready to go?"

She nodded. "Where's Mary?"

"Waiting for us." DeeDee pointed to the door, where Mary stood.

"Are you okay?" Jessica asked, slipping her hand through Kaylee's arm.

"Yes, I'm good." She allowed them to lead her out, her brain working overtime to connect pieces that didn't even seem to be part of the same puzzle.

Her friends couldn't wait to pounce on her once they were safely out of earshot of the attendees.

"What did Christopher say?" Jessica hissed.

"He had to go back to his funeral home on Monday," Kaylee replied. "He wasn't even here when his father was killed."

DeeDee whistled. "Well, that takes him out of the running."

Which leaves one person in the running, Kaylee thought grimly.

As she reached her car, she realized what it was that had been bothering her. "Hey, DeeDee?"

DeeDee paused at Jessica's passenger door. "Yeah?"

"Your DIY series that you've been teaching. Did you mention that you did one class about wildflowers?"

"I did. We took a short hike through some of the woods where I knew a lot of different flowers and plants lived. It was out in the mountain preserve." DeeDee cocked her head.

"Why do you ask?"

"Just curious," Kaylee said, then changed the subject. "I'll call you both tomorrow."

Then Kaylee and Mary climbed into the car.

"You have that look," Mary said, glancing at her.

"I know," Kaylee said, starting the ignition. "I really believe Nathan might have done this. It makes sense."

"Why do you think so?"

As Kaylee drove out of the parking lot, she ticked points off on one hand while using the other to steer. "He had access to Mitchum and the park all day Monday. He knew Giles was tied up. He knew Jay had fought with Mitchum already, giving him a perfect setup. He also had a history with Mitchum, and he might have been a partner in some of his business dealings. He may have stood to lose a lot of money if some deal was going wrong."

"It certainly sounds bad," Mary agreed. "But the sheriff is going to have to work really hard to prove all this."

"I know. I hope Jay shows up soon and with an alibi. At least that will narrow the suspect field," Kaylee said.

When they reached Mary's house, Mary leaned over and hugged Kaylee tightly. "Please be careful. I don't like this. Not one bit."

"I don't like it either. But someone has to get to the bottom of it." Kaylee waved toward the porch, where Herb had come out the front door and stood watching them. "Someone's waiting for you."

"I wish you had someone waiting at home for you. I worry about you."

"There's no need to worry. I'm fine. Go on," Kaylee said, nudging her friend. "Hopefully I'll have good news for you in the morning."

She watched until Mary and Herb had gone inside, arms

around each other.

Kaylee couldn't get home fast enough. It had been a long, stressful day, and she couldn't wait to relax in the cottage with Bear at her side. She needed quiet time for her brain to process everything she'd seen and heard tonight, and she hoped she'd be able to figure out how all of it might fit together.

Kaylee thought back to that Monday. Nathan had been involved at least peripherally in the dinner event. He would have known when everyone would be on-site and when he'd have his moment alone with Mitchum. She'd wondered why Jay's car hadn't looked like anyone but Jay had been in it. Maybe Nathan had driven Mitchum to the park under the guise of being part of the setup so he could poison him.

She shuddered as she pulled into her driveway. But why? What did Nathan have against Mitchum? Unless everything went back to whatever sketchy business deal he had been talking about outside the restaurant with Nolan. What if Nathan had been part of Mitchum's crew? Maybe he decided he wasn't getting a big enough cut and that he'd get a bigger piece of the pie if the boss was out of the way. Or maybe he felt slighted by Mitchum's lack of interest in his business.

Kaylee had no idea how any of that would work, but if they were doing something illegal, anything could have happened.

What if Jay was in trouble? What if he'd stumbled upon the scene with Mitchum and Nathan, and Nathan had realized he couldn't have any witnesses? She swallowed. She couldn't follow that train of thought. It was too horrible.

An even more insidious thought crept up on her. Had Jay and Nathan been in on the murder together? If they were, what did that mean? And where was Jay now?

It was all too much. She just wanted to get inside, lock her house up tight, and cuddle with Bear.

Kaylee had to call Maddox. There was no guarantee that he would investigate her leads, but she had to tell him what she had found out and what she had guessed. If he'd only listen to her, then she could let him take it from there and figure it out.

She felt extremely vulnerable out here, sitting alone in her driveway, so she grabbed her phone and jumped out of the car.

Kaylee stopped and scanned the area around her house. She'd left her porch light on, but it didn't completely chase away the deep shadows that threatened to swallow her up. Taking a deep breath, she squared her shoulders and marched toward the front door.

Suddenly, Bear started barking furiously from inside the cottage.

She flinched, then sprinted toward the door.

Right before she reached it, a figure emerged from the shadows.

Kaylee froze.

The figure moved swiftly into the light reflected off the porch. "Sorry. I didn't mean to frighten you. It's just me."

"Jay, you're all right! What are you doing here?" Kaylee asked, relief quickly replacing her fear. Impulsively, she gave him a brief hug, then held him at arm's length to examine him. "Where have you been? We've all been so worried."

"I'm sorry. I didn't know where else to go. Can we talk inside? I need to confide in someone I can trust." He glanced around, as if he felt exposed. "You have to believe me. I didn't kill anyone." His voice broke on the last words.

"I do believe you. Come in. We have a lot to discuss." She unlocked the door and scooped up Bear, who finally stopped barking and wagged his tail at the sight of his friend.

Jay followed her inside.

Kaylee led him to the kitchen, flipping on lights and trying to decide what to do. "Do you know how many people are searching for you?"

"My parents must be worried sick."

"They are," Kaylee confirmed, her tone stern.

Jay dropped into a chair and put his head in his hands. "I've made such a mess of everything. I don't know what to do or where to go. Please help me."

Kaylee studied her friend. He was certainly desperate and disheveled, but he still didn't look like a killer to her. "Do you need something to eat or drink?"

"Please. Just water and maybe a sandwich? It's been a long time since I had any good food."

She set Bear down, and the dog immediately plopped himself at Jay's feet. Bear seemed to sense that Jay was in need of comfort.

Kaylee retrieved a glass from the cupboard, filled it with ice and water, and handed it to Jay. Then she went to the fridge and took out ingredients to make him a turkey sandwich. She glanced at his drawn face and decided to make that sandwich as thick as she could.

Kaylee knew she should have called Maddox immediately, and she'd probably catch all kinds of grief from him when he found out about this. She might be crazy for entertaining Jay, but she couldn't turn her back on a friend.

"For starters, you should go see Maddox." She set the plate on the table in front of him. "You have to turn yourself in."

"Thank you," Jay said, picking up the sandwich. He took a huge bite. "But I can't go to Maddox. He'll arrest me."

"I'm the last person who would think you had anything to do with it," Kaylee said. "But you were at the park, you took off after Mitchum was killed, and you've been missing ever since. It looks bad for you."

"I know," he said grimly. "He wanted it that way, and I played right into his hands."

Kaylee slid into the chair across from him. "Who wanted it that way?"

"Nathan."

She sat back, her heart pounding. "I knew it," she said, but she felt anything but triumphant. "I just knew it."

He stared at her. "What are you talking about?"

"We have to call Maddox." Kaylee grabbed her phone.

"Wait." Jay held out a hand. "Maddox isn't going to run over there and arrest Nathan for murder. Not after the way Nathan's been positioning me. And what do you mean, you knew it?"

"I'd suspected, but tonight I figured it out. Nathan's been lying about Seamus and you."

"Me? What's he been saying about me?"

"All kinds of stuff," Kaylee replied. "He told me Mitchum was blackmailing you, and you didn't want to take over your dad's business anymore."

"When did he say all of that?" Jay asked, incredulous.

"I've been asking questions over the past couple of days. I wanted to know if Mitchum was trying to buy Nathan out and if there was some problem that could have resulted in the murder. Your dad also told me that Mitchum wanted to buy his place."

Jay seemed to fold in on himself, as if the anger had been sucked out of him. "I know."

"You do? How?"

"I was supposed to be Mitchum's escort during the entire convention. My father wanted someone to keep an eye on Mitchum, and he wanted me engaged. But Dad had no idea that Mitchum was trying to get me to work for him. He wanted to get to my father through me."

19

"Mitchum wanted you to work for him? Where?" Kaylee's mind reeled. There was way too much information coming at her at once.

"At whatever local funeral home he decided to snap up," Jay answered. "Maybe even my own father's place. But the bottom line is, he wanted my dad's business. And he thought if he got me on board, my dad would cave and sell it to him."

"But your dad was seriously considering Mitchum's offer," Kaylee said.

Jay laughed. "Where did you hear that ridiculous rumor?"

"Your dad," Kaylee said.

Jay's smile faded. "My dad told you that?"

"Yes."

He shoved his plate away, suddenly pale. "It's because of me, isn't it?"

"Your dad didn't say it like that," Kaylee said gently. "He felt that if you didn't want the business, he didn't see a reason to keep it."

"Great," Jay said. "So now I'm responsible for destroying my family's legacy too. Dad must be crushed."

"You can't think of it that way. Your father only wants you to be happy. He won't make you do something you don't want to do," Kaylee said. "But first, we need to clear your name. We have to tell Maddox what we know. Tell me what happened Monday."

Jay picked up his water and took a sip. "I was supposed to take Mitchum to the party, and Nathan offered to do it for me.

After our argument in the café, I guess word got around that Mitchum and I weren't getting along."

"What was that about?" Kaylee asked.

"Mitchum wanted me to commit to working for him. He offered me a ton of money and an impressive title. I think he hoped he could make a big announcement here at the convention, embarrass my father, the whole bit. I couldn't take it anymore and walked out."

"When did Nathan offer to drive Mitchum to the park?"

"A little later, Nathan caught up with me and told me he'd take care of chauffeuring him around for the rest of the day. He said it looked like I needed some space."

"Did he ask why you two were fighting?"

Jay nodded. "I just told him Mitchum was treating me like his servant and I was done putting up with it, which was technically true."

"Why didn't you tell Nathan what was really going on?" Kaylee asked.

"I didn't trust him. Something just seemed off, you know? Anyway, Nathan said I was being immature and sensitive. Who knows? He could have been aware of the whole thing and was only putting on an act."

"Nathan thought sometimes it was easier for you to talk to him than your dad," Kaylee said. "He said you confided in him all the time."

Jay gave a bitter laugh. "Of course he'd say that. That way it wouldn't sound weird when he told everyone how screwed up I was. After all, he would know if he was close to me. Add murder suspect to the list, and no one had a hard time believing it, right?"

Kaylee grabbed his arm. "No, that's not true. I've been telling anyone who'll listen that you didn't have anything to do with the murder. Mary and everyone else who knows you are also on your side. But the longer you stayed gone, the harder it was for people to believe you're innocent."

"I get it. Really, I do."

"People are also talking about your arrest for fighting, using it as proof that you're capable of violence. What happened at the bar?"

"It was a terrible mistake." Jay hung his head. "I met someone there, and we were hitting it off. Then a guy came over and started bothering her, and I went a little overboard in trying to protect her. I was so frustrated with everything else that was going on, and I let it get the best of me."

"Why did you stay away? Why didn't you call your parents? They've been so worried."

"Because Nathan knows I know that he murdered Mitchum," Jay said. "I didn't want to put them in any danger. If he thought I was talking, he'd want to get rid of me and anyone I'd talked to so he could cover his tracks."

"But why would Nathan want to kill Mitchum?" Kaylee asked. "Were they working together?"

"I have no idea. Your guess for his motive is as good as mine. I just know what happened," Jay said. "But I wasn't as friendly with Nathan as he tried to make it sound. Honestly, I didn't even like him."

"Your dad said as much. It was one of the reasons I knew Nathan was lying," Kaylee said. "So go on. You got to the party, and then what happened?"

"Yeah. I had to oversee the setup. When I arrived, Nathan and Mitchum were already there, but they didn't see me. No one else was around when I watched them go into the tent together. I couldn't hear what they were saying."

Kaylee leaned forward. "Could you guess?"

"I think they were arguing because they both sounded angry, but I couldn't make out what it was about. Given what

Mitchum was doing to me, I guessed they might be trying to double-cross my father."

"I would have thought the same thing."

"I tried to get closer to the tent so I could pick up their conversation," he said. "Before I could, Nathan walked out. He spotted me before I could duck behind a tree. After he left, I stayed there and waited, but Mitchum never came out."

"What did you do then?" Kaylee asked.

"I wasn't sure what was going on, so I kept waiting," Jay responded. "Finally, I went for a short walk to try to pull myself together. When I got back, I saw the emergency vehicles and heard Mitchum was dead. Someone mentioned that I had been there, but no one knew where I was. I freaked out and took off."

"So where have you been all this time?"

"I mostly stayed in the woods," Jay answered.

"These woods?" Kaylee gestured to the window, thinking of the light she'd seen in the woods last night. "Really?"

He nodded. "I didn't know what to do. I did try to do some detective work, though."

"What do you mean?" Kaylee asked.

"Well, I was trying to keep an eye on my dad. And I tried to call you to tell you earlier. I didn't know who else to call, and I thought maybe you could find out some information for me."

"You were my mysterious caller," Kaylee said. "Whose phone did you use? I didn't recognize the number."

"I paid a teenager who was hiking in the woods to let me borrow his phone. But the service was really bad, and I couldn't hear anything you were saying. I'm guessing it was the same for you."

"When you called, I was at the restaurant where the funeral directors were. I assumed the reception issue was on my end, so I went outside to get a better signal. I ended up overhearing

Nathan out there with Nolan. It sounded like they were talking about a deal."

"What kind of deal?"

"I don't know, but I heard Nolan say Mitchum's death wasn't part of the plan."

"Guess the plan went awry," Jay said.

They sat in silence for a minute.

Kaylee attempted to control her racing thoughts. "We really need to call the sheriff," she said.

"I promise I'll call Maddox, but I have to see my dad first," Jay said. "In case I wind up in jail, I need to tell him I didn't do anything."

She knew she'd want to do the same thing in Jay's shoes. Although she had every intention of helping him convince Maddox that Nathan was the culprit.

"Come on," she said, standing up. "Let's go see your dad."

When they arrived at Akin Funeral Chapel, the building was dark. It didn't seem that odd to Kaylee, since it was nearly one o'clock in the morning.

She pulled into the driveway. "Do you have a key?"

Jay nodded. He led her around to the side door and unlocked it, pausing when he pushed it open.

"What's wrong?" Kaylee asked from behind him.

"I don't know," Jay whispered. "I thought I heard something."

"Is your dad up and around?" she suggested.

"No idea." Jay put his finger to his lips and motioned her inside after him.

Kaylee thought it was kind of creepy to be sneaking around

a dark funeral home in the middle of the night, but what choice did she have?

They passed through the main area, where Kaylee and Christopher had shared coffee earlier that evening. It had been only a few hours ago, but Kaylee felt as if it had been weeks.

Kaylee stuck close to Jay, hoping her eyes would adjust. She was beginning to feel suffocated in the darkness.

As Jay reached the staircase, he finally flipped on a light.

A voice behind them said quietly, "Hello, Jay. I knew you'd come out of hiding eventually."

Kaylee turned to find Abby Anghelone, Nathan's wife, standing there. She appeared calm and put together. Except she held a gun.

Kaylee froze, feeling all the blood drain from her face.

Beside her, Jay sprang into action, lunging toward Abby with his arms outstretched as if to grab the gun.

Abby pointed the pistol square at him. "Don't move."

He stopped. "Where's my dad?"

"I had to secure him for the time being, but he's fine." Abby inclined her head toward Giles's office without taking her eyes off Jay and Kaylee. "He's sitting right in there. Say hi, Giles."

"Son! Thank goodness you're okay!" Giles called out. "I'm here. I'm all right." He was being held captive inside his own office.

"Why don't you leave him alone?" Jay snapped at Abby. "Just let him go. Unless your husband is planning to poison him too."

Abby smiled. "Actually, that was my experiment." She turned to Kaylee. "The class your friend teaches is very thorough and well worth the money."

Kaylee felt sick. "What's going on? What are you talking about?"

"I guess you're not as smart as I thought," Abby sneered. "I figured you'd have the whole thing put together by now. You've certainly been inquisitive enough."

"Enlighten me," Kaylee said.

"I poisoned Mitchum," Abby said smugly.

"You?" Jay asked. "But I saw Nathan in the tent with him. Nathan walked away, but Mitchum never came back out."

"When Nathan left the tent, I went in and gave Mitchum a drink," Abby explained. "It was my very own concoction."

Kaylee couldn't stop staring at Abby as it all came together in her mind. Jay had heard Nathan and Mitchum arguing in the tent, and then he saw Nathan leave. He must have been out walking when Abby slipped inside and killed Mitchum.

"Does Nathan know about this?" Kaylee asked.

Abby shook her head. "He would have tried to talk me out of it. I didn't want him to know. I followed them out to the park and chose the perfect moment."

"Why did you do it?" Jay asked.

"We were about to lose everything—our business, our livelihood, and even our house." Abby raised her chin. "I couldn't let it happen."

"Was Nathan working for Mitchum?" Kaylee asked.

"Yes, he had been for years. Mitchum always told Nathan he was the son he never had. His own son was quite useless, as you've no doubt heard." Abby laughed, but it was a chilling sound.

"What did Nathan do for Mitchum?" Kaylee persisted.

"Mitchum hired Nathan and several other people to find funeral homes and offer to buy them in different areas. But Nathan was the smartest one of the bunch." Her voice rang with pride.

"Then how were you about to lose everything?" Jay asked.

"Nathan did everything for Mitchum. He closed deals, and he handled Mitchum's crazy business partners." Abby scoffed. "Including Nolan."

"So Nathan was doing a deal with him," Kaylee said.

"Of course he was," Abby snapped. "Nathan had to help that

big dolt figure out how to get it done. They were about to close on it, but then some lawyer threw a wrench into the works. So Nathan had to figure that out too. But despite everything Nathan did for Mitchum, he wasn't getting the money he deserved."

Jay opened his mouth, but Kaylee put a hand on his arm. When he looked at her, she slowly shook her head. They needed to stall Abby and hope an opportunity to get out of this mess would present itself.

"Nathan knew Mitchum wanted to branch out here, and he offered to lead the acquisition," Abby went on. "Nathan created a plan for all the funeral homes on this side of the state, including ours. He knew Mitchum would help expand it in a way he never could on his own. Mitchum had the money, the resources, and the connections Nathan lacked."

"So why did you kill Mitchum? It's pretty hard to be partners with a dead guy," Kaylee said. She casually slipped her hand into her pocket and felt for her phone, which had an emergency call button on the lock screen. Maybe she could call 911 without Abby noticing.

"You didn't let me finish," Abby said with a smile, but Kaylee could see a glint of menace in her eyes.

Kaylee pressed the home button on her phone to activate the screen, then poked the bottom left corner, praying she'd dialed emergency. She hoped she had the volume down enough that Abby wouldn't hear when the dispatcher answered. If she'd even made the call.

"I won't bore you with all the details, but Mitchum liked Nathan's proposal. Except for our own funeral home," Abby said bitterly. "He didn't think it was worth the money. After he'd wooed us with figures for years while he got Nathan's help on everything else, he turned us down."

"What happened then?" Jay asked.

"Nathan wanted to run your father's place with Mitchum's backing," Abby said. "But there were two problems. Our dear friend Giles didn't want to sell to Mitchum, and Mitchum refused to make Nathan a full partner, even though Nathan could have gotten Giles to sell. Mitchum would only agree to letting Nathan manage this place with a cut, which meant we still didn't get the money we deserve. The money we needed, with Nathan working for Mitchum for a fraction of what he deserved all these years," she added, desperation in her voice.

"That's terrible," Kaylee said sympathetically. *Keep talking, Abby.*

"We were about to lose everything," Abby said. "But if Mitchum was gone, Nathan would be in a much better position. The other partners all love Nathan. It was Mitchum that was holding him back." It sounded like she was talking about making the decision to accept one job over another instead of taking a man's life.

Kaylee gaped at her. "But you . . . what about your children? You have kids!" she exclaimed.

"You act like I'm going to get caught," Abby replied. "The only person who was there when it happened was Jay. And I'm going to take care of that loose end tonight. He was having a lot of problems," she said with a knowing look at Jay.

Kaylee still couldn't believe what she was hearing. "What are you planning to do with us?"

Abby grinned at Kaylee. "Jay came back here and killed his father and you and then himself. He couldn't get caught, you see. You just had to keep poking around, didn't you? Even though everything my husband told you about Jay should have pointed you in another direction."

"Nathan was spreading all those lies about me," Jay said. "If he wasn't in on this with you, why did he do it?"

"He blamed you when your father refused to sell his company

to Mitchum," Abby replied, "and he wanted a little revenge. That was an added benefit for me and my plan. He set it up very nicely," she said with a small smile.

Kaylee's mind was reeling. "Nathan tried to get revenge on Jay by incriminating him, but why did he lie to me about knowing Seamus?"

"Nathan felt terrible about what Mitchum did to Seamus's father," Abby said. "He didn't want anyone to know that Seamus had a connection to him or Mitchum because Seamus was a suspect. Nathan was trying to protect him."

Kaylee didn't know what to say.

"But it was all your fault, Jay," Abby went on, her voice taking on a hint of hysteria. "Giles kept hesitating to sell the business because of you, and you don't even want it."

Kaylee could almost feel Jay's anger radiating off him in waves. *Please don't do anything stupid,* she begged silently. "Why did you think I would believe Jay was guilty?" she asked Abby. "He's my friend."

The other woman shrugged. "I figured if I could get you to think Jay was unstable and that he'd been angry enough at Mitchum to want him dead, you'd leave the whole thing alone. But you never did, so unfortunately you're going to end up collateral damage."

Abby was seriously going to kill them all and blame it on Jay. Kaylee felt light-headed. She staggered back and sank down on one of the steps.

Abby watched her with a victorious glint in her eye.

The second Abby took her gaze off him, Jay sprang forward and tackled her. The gun hit the floor.

Kaylee flung herself toward the gun just as Abby wriggled free of Jay and reached for it. Kaylee managed to shove the gun farther from the other woman. It spun away on the smooth floor.

As Abby tried to scramble away to retrieve the gun, Kaylee grabbed the woman's ankles, and she fell flat just shy of the weapon. Kaylee scrambled to her feet and darted past Abby as she lay prone.

Giles yelled something from the office.

In that split second, Abby went for her gun once more.

Kaylee knocked the other woman over again. "Please stay down," she said.

Abby snarled up at her from the floor, but she didn't move.

Jay went into the office to free his father. Giles called 911 while Jay restrained Abby.

The front door burst open, and Sheriff Maddox and Deputies Durham and Garcia entered, guns drawn, yelling for everyone to freeze.

Kaylee turned to Maddox. "Don't even think about touching Jay. He didn't do anything."

"Relax," Maddox said, raising his hands. "This is why I didn't want you in on the case. I knew you and Jay were close, and I didn't want you to feel like you were betraying your friend if the evidence pointed to him."

"Oh," Kaylee said in a small voice. She had to admire that he'd considered her feelings in the matter. She quickly explained what had happened.

Nick slapped handcuffs on Abby, then led her outside to the patrol car.

The sheriff appeared disgusted as he watched them go. "Three little ones at home and she goes out and poisons her husband's boss."

Giles embraced his son. "I was so worried," he said.

Jay hugged him back. "Where's Mom? Is she okay?"

Giles nodded. "Thankfully she was visiting one of her friends tonight. I would have been beside myself if she'd been here for this."

"Dad, I'm so sorry," Jay said. "This is all my fault."

"Hardly," Giles said. "This was the product of greedy men." He turned to Kaylee. "Thank you."

"For what?" she asked.

"For believing in my son when not many other people did."

"The whole town loves you guys," Kaylee said. "No one wanted to believe Jay had done anything wrong."

"Well, I hope no one thinks that anymore. I wouldn't want it to hurt business," Jay said. "Since I'm going to be depending on this place for my livelihood and all."

Kaylee and Giles both stared at him.

"You mean it?" Giles asked hesitantly, as if he were almost afraid of the answer.

"I mean it. And when I take over, I want people to have as much faith in me as they have in you."

Kaylee beamed as father and son embraced once more.

20

"Well," Jessica said, "it's certainly been an exciting week around here."

"You can say that again," Kaylee replied.

The Petal Pushers, along with their honorary member Bear and special guest Reese, were all out to dinner. They'd gone to O'Brien's, so Bear could be part of the festivities too.

It was a beautiful night on the island. The water glistened a lovely blue-green beyond them. The tide was low, sending small waves crashing lightly over the sand. A warm breeze ruffled their napkins.

Kaylee felt relaxed for the first time in days, and she actually had an appetite.

"Hear! Hear!" Mary said, lifting her glass in a toast.

DeeDee followed suit.

Kaylee turned to Reese. "I'm glad we finally got to do dinner this week."

"I'm glad you're alive to do dinner," Reese said. He sounded serious.

Kaylee smiled at him. "Me too. What a relief it's over."

Jessica nodded. "Seriously, Kaylee, when we heard what happened . . ." She shook her head. "We were all so worried. Taking on a madwoman with a gun like that? You're really brave."

"Or really crazy," DeeDee chimed in.

Kaylee laughed. "Come on, guys. You would've done the same."

"No way," DeeDee said promptly. "As soon as Jay pounced, I would have raced into the office with Giles and locked the door until someone came to help."

"It's probably good that Kaylee didn't do that," Mary mused. "Abby could have shot Jay and escaped. Then where would we be?"

"It's lucky we went to see Giles," Kaylee said. "Bringing Jay there forced all this out into the open. And Abby confessed to everything, which the police thankfully managed to record during my 911 call. I got the distinct impression that she was even proud of what she had done. How insane is that?" She took a sip of water. "I think she truly believed she was going to get away with it."

"I feel so guilty," DeeDee said soberly. "I gave her a lot of information on poisonous flowers."

"You can't look at it that way," Mary said. "It had nothing to do with you. She's a very troubled woman, and she would have found a way to do it with or without your class."

DeeDee let out a deep breath. "I feel terrible for her poor husband and children."

"I know," Kaylee said. "It's so awful. How can Nathan explain to their children what happened? And imagine what those kids will go through for the rest of their lives."

"Abby seemed so nice," Jessica said.

"Did Christopher go home?" DeeDee asked.

"Yes, I saw him leave this morning," Jessica answered.

"Is he going to take over his dad's business?" DeeDee asked.

Jessica nodded. "That's what he told me. He's still dealing with his dad's death, but he seemed pretty optimistic about managing the business. I think he'll do just fine."

"I'm so glad his dad's death was solved," Kaylee continued. "Thankfully the right person is behind bars, and Giles and Jay can get on with figuring out their lives and running their business together, like Giles always wanted them to."

"Thelma is over the moon," Mary said. "She's so relieved to have her son back home."

"That's great. And now everyone else can get back to their lives," Reese said. He grinned at Kaylee. "A few normal days might do you some good."

Kaylee thought about that. "It might feel nice to sleep through the night without waking up wondering who the killer is," she admitted.

"Definitely." Jessica sighed. "We've had enough excitement around here for the rest of the year, I think."

"Oh, I don't know about that," Kaylee said. "I mean, the funeral convention isn't even over yet. You never know what might happen next in Turtle Cove."

Up to this point, we've been doing all the writing. Now it's *your* turn!

Tell us what you think about this book, the characters, the bad guy, or anything else you'd like to share with us about this series. We can't wait to hear from *you*!

Log on to give us your feedback at:

https://www.surveymonkey.com/r/FlowerShopMysteries

Annie's® FICTION